ONE

"You're *benching* me!" Orla Nyrén spat, furious and disbelieving at the same time. "No," she said. "It's not happening. You can't treat me like a child. I'm not having it."

Sir Charles Wyndham sighed and shook his head. "It's not like that," he said, wheeling his chair around the table to where she sat. The other chairs, one each for Ronan Frost, Noah Larkin, Konstantin Khavin, and Jude Lethe, were empty. This was a private conversation. A quiet word. Now she knew why.

Jude, the only other person in the room, stood beside the line of first editions in a book case, feigning a keen interest in *A Tale of Two Cities.* It was obvious he wanted to be anywhere but there.

"It's mandatory leave."

"There's a difference?"

"Of course there is, woman. The entire team is standing down. Two weeks. No crises. It's a well deserved rest. It's not a punishment, Orla. It's a reward."

"I don't want to rest. I want to do *something.*"

"I know you do, but you're not doing it alone. Right now Ronan is in the south of France. Konstantin says he's visiting a friend – though let's be honest, I doubt very much that he has

1

any – and Noah is... Noah is doing whatever the hell Noah does on his downtime. I've learned not to ask."

"And Jude?"

"Oh, I'm on holiday," the tech wizard with *Joe 90* glasses replied. "Can't you tell? I'm totally chilled. This is me on vacation." He put the book back on the shelf. Out of place.

The old man didn't comment on it. Instead, he said, "After his experiences in Peru, Mr Lethe has opted to vacation here at the luxurious Nonesuch Hotel." Sir Charles chuckled to himself over his little joke.

Orla didn't so much as crack a smile. "I thought you'd brought me in to give me a new assignment."

"You only just got back from Poland!"

"The key word there is *back*. I did a damn fine job. Notice the past tense. Did. As in Done. Done as in finished. Over."

"Nobody is disputing that," the old man said.

"Koni and Ronan did have to fly in to help," Jude noted.

Orla shook her head. "There was no 'have to' about it, the old man got antsy, but I had everything under control," Orla insisted. "By the time they arrived it was all over bar the shouting."

"Orla, please, nobody doubts your unique talents, my dear. It would be remiss of me if I were to ignore your needs as a human being though. Everyone needs to decompress. Especially after what you have been through over there. And since you will not take a holiday voluntarily, I simply had to insist you take one, starting now. No arguments, my dear. I won't be persuaded otherwise."

Orla sat quietly. She wasn't going to win this. The old man had a habit of getting his way. She *was* tired, though she would never admit that out loud.

"Where the hell am I going to go?"

"Not Peru," said Jude.

ARGO

BOOK SIX OF

THE
OGMIOS
DIRECTIVE

STEVEN SAVILE
AND ASHLEY KNIGHT

000002103957

Proudly published by Snowbooks

Copyright © 2017 Steven Savile & Ashley Knight

Steven Savile and Ashley Knight assert the moral
right to be identified as the authors of this work.
All rights reserved.

Snowbooks Ltd | email: info@snowbooks.com
www.snowbooks.com.

British Library Cataloguing in Publication Data.
A catalogue record for this book is available from the
British Library. Paperback / softback

ISBN: 978-1-911390-28-2

First published April 2017

Secret Service Mandate 7266, otherwise known as the Ogmios Directive, sanctioned the formation of an elite team under the command of Sir Charles Wyndham. Their orders are to do anything and everything necessary to preserve the sovereignty of the British Isles. What that actually means is difficult to pin down. They are deniable. They act outside the law, removed from the security of the State.

If something went wrong they were on their own.

If something went right no one ever said thank you.

It was enough that when things went to hell, they were there. Sir Charles, known affectionately to his people as the old man, calls them the Forge Team, but their nickname amongst themselves is the Lost Cause.

They serve at the pleasure of Her Majesty and report to a faceless bureaucrat in the upper echelons of government known only as Control, though no one with the power to would ever admit that.

These five men and women are often the last hope.

"And not the Middle East," Sir Charles said. "You'll only get embroiled in something messy and exhausting. We had thoughts."

"Did you now?"

"A nice Greek island," Jude said, putting the tickets on the table in front of her.

"Okay, whatever. You've obviously thought this through."

Jude crossed the room to a second bookshelf, this one stacked with fake books that concealed a secret door. Behind it was a lift that led down to the nest, the nerve-centre of the entire Ogmios operation. The nest was Jude's lair. He designed every inch of it. He had a bedroom in the manor, but hadn't slept a single night in his bed. "You know," Jude said as he stepped into the lift, "one day I'm going to get my wish and have a fireman's pole installed."

Orla and Sir Charles ignored him.

"You know you'd want to slide down my pole," he said, and then he was gone, the shelf sliding back in place.

"All you have to do is have fun, Orla. Relax, you've earned it."

Orla let out a long breath.

"Okay," she said.

"I had your bags packed. Do try to get yourself to the airport before your flight leaves. Oh and it goes without saying, but I'll say it anyway, try not to cause an international incident when you're out there. We don't want any dead bodies washing up on stony beaches or anything."

"I'll do my best," she said. "But I'm not making any promises."

TWO

It began with a steady beat. She focussed on it. She gritted her teeth, not in pain. The rhythm was there. It came in undulating waves, bouncing off the cracked whitewashed wall of the hotel room. The build-up promised an escape. A way out of life. Out of her own head. At least for a moment. That was all she needed.

Orla's fingers dug into the Egyptian cotton sheets, clawing at the mattress. She arched, her neck stretching, pushing her head backward, deep into the sweat-matted feathers of her pillow, until she could feel him everywhere. His breath was ragged in her ear. The sweat clung to their skins like glue, bodies peeling apart as they fucked. It wasn't gentle. It wasn't love-making or anything like it. It was pure. Carnal. Overwhelming. And for just a few seconds at least, it promised to keep the darkness at bay.

Her entire body quivered.

Every muscle tensed.

Every tendon strung taut.

She reached around, grasping the bare cheeks of his arse, sinking her nails in deep even as he bucked against the sudden flare of pain, and forced him in balls deep and refused to let him out again as he came.

Her own orgasm was deep-rooted and fierce. Her entire being was reduced, for the silence between one breath and the next, as the air caught in her lungs. Her existence was caught in that moment. And then the cry tore out of her, reverent, religious, and relief swept through her, spent.

"Orla." He found his voice. It was a good voice. Deep. Soft. Rich. A good man's voice. Even in that one word, just her name, his accent was thick. Strong fingers gripped her waist. He refused to let himself slip out of her, breaking the moment, but eventually he fell to his side, his hand pulling her with him. She allowed herself to be held. It wasn't her. She wasn't a cuddling up, whisper-sweet-nothings kind of girl. She was a cigarette and a contented sigh kind of woman, taking pride in a shag well shagged.

"I love you," he whispered.

The beat of his heart drummed against her back.

"No you don't," she said.

"I do," he said.

They weren't the words she wanted to hear.

Untangling herself from his arms, she slipped across the bed and dangled her legs over the side. She stared at the wall. A crack ran from the tiled floor to the ceiling, like a snake slithering upward, or downward, depending on your perspective. "I told you, I won't fall in love with you."

"I know," he answered. "But I made no such promise."

"You don't know." The memories slid back into place – a black stain smearing the moment. Everything that had happened her. Her ghosts. They were always there. And they always fucked with intimacy. "You can't know."

"You're right: I know nothing. I don't know you at all. But I *want* to."

Orla stood, not concerned that the open windows would leave her exposed to any passerby who happened to look up. She reached for the crack in the wall and ran her finger along it.

"This is me," she said. "This crack. You want to know me, this is what I am. Broken, and I'll never be fixed."

"Let me try."

She turned and faced him. He lay on his back watching her. He'd made no move to cover himself, even as he softened. His skin was golden. His muscles might as well have been carved in marble.

"You deserve someone better," she began.

He shook his head.

"No. I deserve you."

"Bullshit," she said. "I'm not some trophy that gets handed out for being a good boy. And trust me, if you had me, you wouldn't want me after a week or a month. My life doesn't work like that."

His smile faded. "I want you to be my eternity."

There were no words, but instead of leaving, as she had always done in the past, she hesitated. Still naked, still slick with their comingled sweat. There was no such a thing as the fairy tale. Pretty words faded soon enough, the silences stretched out, and eventually there was nothing left to say except for goodbye. But that didn't change the fact that deep down, on some subconscious level, she needed to be held. Just for a while. Just for today. Maybe tomorrow.

"Come back to bed," he said, holding out his arm, his body responding.

She hesitated, looking at his hand and hardness behind it, had in that moment, the broken pieces of her called out loud enough for Orla to ignore her better judgment. She took his hand and allowed herself to be pulled back into bed.

"I have waited many lifetimes to find you," he whispered, serious sea green eyes searching hers for something. "I offer you my soul."

"Just fuck me," she said, but even that bluntness couldn't mask the fact that she was thinking about letting herself fall. Just this once. Just for a few days. Just to be normal for a while.

THREE

The night she met Ares was her first in Corinth.

A desperate need to be around *life* had driven her to pull on the red dress and walk down the road to the small bar. She had no intention beyond taking up a new address at Number One, The End Of The Bar, and drink until Poland was out of her head, and the voices of Jenin were drowned out. There was no nightlife to speak of in Corinth. But there was noise and distraction. That had to be enough. Remembering the old man's orders, she left her gun in her room. Habit said, take it. Instinct said, take it. In the end she decided to embrace the concept of normality, even if only for a night. She secured the firearm in the room's small lockbox in the bottom of the wardrobe.

Being alone had transformed into loneliness in a single day. It was different being out here on her own without a job.

She heard him before she saw him.

She was at the door to the bar when his shout rang out from down the dark alleyway alongside the old building. She hesitated. She wasn't in the mood to be sociable, but she wasn't in the mood to be alone, either. Besides, she hadn't dressed for an evening of flying solo.

But the gun would have been nice. Old habits. She walked slowly to the corner, and entered the narrow alley. There was a small parking lot at the back with room for half a dozen cars.

A second shout, louder now she was closer.

She quickened her pace.

An old Ford Cortina was parked in the centre of the small lot. Beside it she saw the shadow of a man, half hidden in the gloom. There were three others in a ring around him. They didn't look like old friends. They were focussed on the messenger bag strapped around his neck. He wasn't giving it up for love nor money, not even when the first man pulled a knife.

Orla kicked off her heels. She moved into the lot silently, padding forward on her bare feet.

They didn't hear her.

The victim had both hands on his attacker's arm, and was struggling to keep the blade from sinking into his gut. He couldn't block a rabbit punch to the kidney from the second mugger.

As the victim twisted, back arching, and opened himself up to the knife edge, Orla stepped in. She disarmed the first man with a blow to the arm so hard she heard his elbow crack. She didn't wait for him to go down. As his cohort spun around, she kicked out and slammed the ball of her heel into his throat. It was brutally effective. He staggered back, clutching at his neck, gasping. The knife skittered away across the clay road.

The first attacker held his victim on the floor, and was putting all of his weight onto the knife trying to drive it down. Orla landed a solid kick to the side of his head, sending him sprawling across the ground. His victim was no longer in immediate danger, but wasn't moving. She didn't have time to check on him. A glint of silver in the moonlight flashed in the corner of her eye. Instinctively, she blocked the knife thrust without seeing who it came from, parrying the weapon aside.

She looked at the third attacker properly.

He was short and stocky, all of his strength in his upper body, like a coiled spring.

Orla read his momentum and used his forward motion against him, sweeping low and pitching him over her head. It was all about maximum efficiency with minimum exertion. Using the opponent's strength against him. Let him do all the work. As he lost his balance, Orla struck, viper-like, with the heel of her hand, connecting with the man's neck. He crashed to ground in a cloudburst of dust. She'd missed the fatal larynx blow by maybe an inch. It was enough to leave him choking in the dirt, neutralised.

The guy with the ruined elbow was on his feet. He ripped out a curse in Greek. Orla stood her ground. He spat at her, then ran away, leaving the first attacker as the last man standing. And he wasn't exactly standing.

On the ground, the victim groaned. It wasn't much of a noise, but it was enough to distract his would-be mugger for the half-second Orla needed to get in close. She brought up an elbow, driving it into his nose. She grabbed his wrist with her free hand, and twisted downwards savagely. The blade fell. She pushed forward, bending the man's arm unnaturally, and continuing to bend it until he screamed, the joint near to rupturing. The old man's admonishment rang in her ears. She didn't go in for the kill, and stopped twisting before the bones snapped. She'd done enough damage.

A knee to the stomach took him out.

He went down hard.

The guy with the ruined elbow was already gone. The guy she'd almost choked to death was on his feet, but he wasn't exactly running, more like stumbling away. The last man scrambled to his feet, blood pouring from his nose. He clutched his injured wrist to his chest with his free hand. He glared at Orla, but didn't stand his ground. He turned tail and ran after his crew of cowards.

Orla let them go.

She dropped to her knees beside their victim.

She pulled his hands away from his side expecting to see blood. His shirt was clean. There was no tear. No blood. He coughed and let out a miserable groan. Orla placed her hands on his torso, working over it as she checked for damage. No broken ribs. Cracked maybe. Bruised definitely.

He gazed up at her, eyes completely unfocussed.

"What happened?" he asked, in Greek. It wasn't one of her primary languages, but she knew enough to understand.

"You were attacked," she said. "Do you speak English?"

"Doesn't everyone?" he said, switching tongues easily.

She helped him to his feet.

He groaned, but with some effort and a little help was able to stand.

"Who were they?" she asked.

He shook his head. "I have no idea. They were after my bag. I tried to tell them there was nothing of value in there, but they wouldn't have it." He looked around, realizing Orla was alone, and trying to work out how she could have dispatched three men on her own.

"What did you do?" He asked. "How?" A second question in a second heartbeat. He couldn't seem to grasp how one woman had saved him. Orla flirted with the idea of the truth, but changed her mind.

"Oh, what? Them? Cowards. I made some noise. It scared them off. They didn't want a fight. They just wanted your bag. When it looked like they might get hurt, they ran."

"Still, you faced down three men. Three men who took me out without blinking an eye. You are an impressive woman, Miss...?" he fished. She smiled. It wasn't just her name he was after; one word would confirm she wasn't married.

"Orla," she said. She held out a hand. "I would say it's nice to meet you, but given the circumstances perhaps something less painful for you would have been better."

"I can live with it," he said. "I'm Ares," he said, taking her hand in both of his. He was stunning, she realised, as the streetlight fell across him: tall and dark, handsome, no not handsome, that was too mundane a word for his beauty. He was *exquisite*. The adrenalin still coursed through her. She wasn't into pretty boys. Never had been. She liked them broken, like her. Like Noah, if she was being honest with herself.

Orla Nyrén was a spy.

She was a killer.

She wasn't a little girl to fall for pretty strangers on balmy nights under foreign skies.

That wasn't who she was.

And yet.

There was something about him.

His eyes.

Sea green.

"Thank you for helping me," he said. "Others wouldn't." He winced and grasped his side again.

"Can you stand on your own?"

"Quite possibly, but it is more fun to lean on you."

"Funny boy. Let's get you to the police station. Do you think you can describe them?"

"No need," he said. "The police here are... not the most... I'm looking for the word."

"Honest?"

"Efficient. It's not worth wasting our time."

"The hospital then?"

He chuckled. "I'm sure a few drinks will fix my wounded pride. Nothing else is badly hurt. I think I owe you a drink. It is the least I can do after everything."

Orla allowed him to let her to guide him into the bar. Sure, he was exaggerating his awkward gait as he made a show of leaning on her some more. Inside, they walked over a sticky floor to the bar. Ares lowered himself onto a stool and nodded to the bartender.

"Tsipouro," he said, resting his hands on the edge of the bar. "And for my hero?"

"Vodka."

A few seconds passed before he slowly turned his head and looked directly at Orla. His gaze softened as he stared. She could read people. It was part and parcel of what she did. She needed to be able to read intent before it became action. That was how she stayed alive. He was thinking about hitting on her. A tiny smile gathered in the corner of his mouth.

"Vodka for the pretty lady," the bartender announced, placing the glass down on the bar. "And Tsipouro for the not so pretty anymore boy."

Ares turned his attention to the drink. Orla watched him savour its aftertaste. She took a swig of her vodka.

"It is not just your preference for English that tells me you're not Greek, right? Your colouration is right, but..." He shrugged, then winced.

"Half Italian," she answered. "And half Swedish," she added.

He nodded as if it was the most obvious genetic blend in the world. "Do you know Tsipouro?"

"Not intimately," Orla said.

"Tsipouro and I are quite close." He picked up the glass. "Do you know how it is made?"

She didn't answer.

He finished the shot. "It was invented by monks in the 14th century."

"Those crazy, drunken monks..."

This time he laughed out loud, his smile brilliant despite the burgeoning bruise. He edged closer to her. "You should really try it."

She shook her head. A fleeting moment of disappointment flickered across his face.

Orla let the silence drag out a few seconds longer than necessary, then cracked a wry smile and shook her head. "Do you always give up so easily?"

He looked at her. "I am not used to rejection," he admitted.

"Where as I am intimately acquainted with it. We're best buds." She realised she was sounding like Noah. "It's always good to get used to disappointment."

"And why is that?"

"Because, my new found friend, our world is full of it."

He watched her reach for her empty shot glass and studied her face as she considered the remnants of vodka left behind.

"You know, when a woman wears red, it only means one thing," he said.

"Sex?"

Again he laughed. A proper, deep, belly laugh. "No! It means you are strong. So tell me, have I figured you out?"

"You'd like to think so, wouldn't you? Tell me, does this work with the Greek girls?"

"I wouldn't know – I've never tried it."

"Liar."

"Not at all. I prefer tourists." Again with that grin. He was painfully sure of himself.

"Okay," she said. "Try me. Let's see if you can crack the enigma that is me."

He set his glass down.

He studied her slowly, letting his gaze linger where it shouldn't. He breathed in deeply. Exhaled slowly. "You are determined, yes? Strong. Not just strong. Fearless. You walked into that alleyway and faced down three men. That is not normal. I think you like to be challenged. It strengthens your resolve. You are resourceful. You drove off three attackers without a weapon. I think you are someone who can be counted on."

"What else?"

"You are beautiful, but that doesn't matter to you. There is a sadness about you, too. You wear it like a veil. Something very bad has happened, I think."

"Cold reading is a clever trick," she said.

He inclined his head. "I am not the smartest man in the world, but I know hurt." He lowered his voice. "And I really do not wish to cause you any more pain. Thank you for helping me. You did not have to. I will not forget that kindness."

He was leaving. Ninety-nine times out of a hundred she'd have pushed him out the door. Tonight was that rare thing, the hundredth.

"I'll let you buy me a drink if you'll let me buy you one," she said.

"I would like that."

"Vodka for monsieur," Orla called.

"Tsipouro for mademoiselle," he said, without breaking eye contact. "I think you'll like it."

"You do? Why?"

"You drink straight vodka." He handed her the shot glass. "To drunken monks," he toasted, raising his glass.

The evening passed quickly, with the two of them wasting the night away with words about nothing and everything. Deep and meaningful, shallow and meaningless, all manner of life, loves, and lost happiness exchanged. And a few of them might even have been true. By two in the morning they were inseparable. Their legs intertwined on the stools, the empty shot glasses lined up in pairs on the bar like the animals boarding Noah's Ark.

The bartender cleared his throat. "Last call for lovers." The shot glasses clinked together as he laced his fingers into them, lifting eight at a time.

Orla sat back on her stool. The clock on the wall told a dirty secret. They'd been at the bar for five hours.

Ares nodded. "Time flies when you're trying to get a pretty girl into bed." He slid from his perch and shouldered his bag.

"Enough with the stupid lines, Ares. They're really not that endearing."

"Then may I walk you to your hotel?"

"It's just down the road. I think I can make it."

"I'm sure you can. Still, may I?" He offered his hand. She stared at it like it was a snake and might somehow rear up to bite her, then slipped her hand into his. This really wasn't her. Moonlight post-Midnight strolls? They walked down the road to the hotel and by the time they reached the huge plate glass doors of the lobby, Orla knew she was going to take him up to her room. He didn't have a choice in the matter, whatever his intentions.

"Will you be safe to go up on your own?"

Orla glanced at him with thinly veiled amusement. "You've got to be kidding me, right? Seriously? Who's the knight in shining armour here?"

Ares chuckled. "You have a point. Perhaps you should escort me back to my hotel?"

"Not a chance. You're coming upstairs."

The elevator ride was painfully slow, the old cogs and gears turning with laboured precision. The carriage shuddered and juddered against the thick steel cables. The five floors took what felt like a lifetime to climb. "No rush," she said, jabbing at the button for her floor again. Ares stepped into her space, his legs straddling hers and pushed her up against the elevator's wall. She didn't fight him. He reached for her face, cupping her cheek and ran his thumb teasingly across her lower lip.

"May I kiss you?" he whispered.

"Enough with the questions. Just do it," she said.

He leaned forward and lightly placed his lips upon hers.

"Better," she said, after he broke away.

He pressed against her mouth and teased the tip of his tongue softly across her parted lips.

She accepted him, his taste sweet and alcoholic, which given her mood was perfect. He pulled her close, his strong hands meeting at the small of her back. Orla sealed what remained of the space between them, leaning in and wrapping her arms around his neck to try to disprove at least one of Newton's laws.

Their breathing quickened as their explorations turned hungry.

She pulled away long enough to steal air.

Ares kissed his way down to her neck.

The intrusive bell chimed their arrival at the fifth floor. The doors parted. They didn't. Beyond lay a low-lit hallway, the subdued lighting pretending at romance. There was nothing romantic in this as the two stumbled out, staggering like drunks as they fumbled their way along the corridor to her room. She struggled with the keycard in the lock, trying to slip it in and out without looking. She swept her hair to the side, pushing the heavy oak door open.

Ares reached down and lifted her into his arms, carrying her into the room.

She laughed at his stupid ideals of male gallantry. This whole powerful male protector thing he had going on was grounded firmly in the 1950s.

She kicked the door closed.

He carried her across the room, his Armani Oxfords echoing off the tiled flooring.

He didn't lay her down on the bed.

He had different ideas.

Better. Nastier. He pushed the red dress up, gathering it at the waist, then pulled it over her head. She reached for his pants, unbuckling his belt with sure fingers.

She stood before him, vulnerable, in a matching red bra and thong. Her flesh had healed since Jenin, but the scars remained, inside and out. This was her. All of her. In that moment, looking over his shoulder at his back and a part of herself in the mirror, memories of the Beast surfaced. She could smell him on her. Those olfactory hallucinations were deep rooted in her amygdala. She would never forget them.

Ares sensed the change in her.

"What's wrong?" he asked. His voice was unsure. Not tender so much as concerned. It brought Orla back to the present.

"Nothing," she lied. She had one purpose now. Escape. She opened his shirt, ripping two of the buttons off in her haste. They rattled on the tiles and rolled away. He possessed the physique of an accomplished swimmer. He wore a gold medallion on a thick chain around his neck, as though showing off his wins in the Olympic pool. She ran her hands over his torso. He removed the necklace and reached for the clip on her bra.

Cupping her breast, he kissed her nipple. She, in turn, placed her arms around his shoulders, pulling him to her. And then he dropped to his knees.

Slipping her panties to the floor, he nudged her legs open and licked her. Then, as she balanced up against the wall, turned her.

There was nothing gentle or tender about their lovemaking, because it wasn't lovemaking in any way, shape or form. It was angry, physical, dirty, pressed up against the wall nails digging into skin, drawing blood, fucking, and it was *good*.

She used him.

He, in turn, was more than willing to be used.

She woke alone.

The sweat-silhouette of his body was stained into her sheets. It was the first time she'd let anyone touch her since the Beast. There had been a moment, in the deepest darkest part of the sweltering night, when he'd been there, the Beast of Jenin, and the floodgates of that hell had threatened to burst open and drown her. But she was in control this time. She owned her body and gave it willingly. That was different. Ares had traced each and every one of her scars but hadn't asked about them. He wasn't interested in their stories. Maybe he didn't even see them as imperfections, not the way that she did.

Self-conscious despite the shared alcohol infused passions, she drew the thin sheet across her nakedness.

The light flutter of fingers on a laptop keyboard drew her attention to the marble table on the far side of the suite where Ares sat with his back to her. He was still naked, but wore that macho-man gold chain about his neck. Beyond him lay the crystal blue waters of the beautiful ocean. He didn't seem the least bit interested in the magnificent view.

She watched him.

The muscles in his back flexed as he leaned forward.

The sunlight blanketing the Gulf of Corinth streamed through the windows, highlighting the motes of dust that danced between them. She saw natural auburn streaks in his black hair.

The night had been exactly what she'd needed. The day brought questions with it. Everyone had a secret. What was his?

Orla wrapped a sheet about her and walked up behind him.

Over his shoulder she saw an intricate map on the screen. It appeared to be watermarked with the faint shape of a ship. The letters 'AI' enclosed within a circle housed the lower left portion of the prints. A leather-bound book filled with notes lay open to his left. He was looking at something written there as she placed a hand on his shoulder. She half-expected him to flinch and close the laptop. He reached up for her hand and tipped his head back, smiling up at her.

"Sleep well?" he asked.

"Had better," she said with a wry smirk. He chuckled.

She nodded to his computer. "Working early?"

"This?" He placed a hand on the top of the screen. "Well, I guess you'd say I'm working on work."

"Working on work?" Maybe it was a translation thing? Something that got lost between one language and the other.

"Why are you still here?" she asked. One night stands weren't supposed to linger. Things that lingered were like bad odours.

"You want me to leave?"

"You can stay," she said. "But I'm hungry. I need breakfast. Worked up a bit of an appetite."

He nodded. "Okay, in answer to your question, I'm here because I want to be." He closed the laptop and turned to face her properly. "I meant what I said last night."

"What part in particular?"

He stood, placing his arms around her and pulling her close. "I love you."

"You're an idiot," she said. "Love doesn't work like that." Meaning I don't love, not now, not after one night, not with some random I saved from getting his arse handed to him on a plate by a bunch of thugs down a dark alleyway.

"Let me prove it to you."

"Bring me coffee, that'd be a start."

"You're a difficult woman," he said

"You think you know me," she said. "You have no idea."

FOUR

The incessant ring of a mobile phone woke Orla.

Ares stirred as she reached over him for it.

She put the phone to her ear. "Hello gorgeous," the voice on the other end was far too chipper.

"Jude?"

"Your one and only."

"To what do I owe the pleasure?"

"You mean I need a reason to call you?"

"When I'm banished from the kingdom? I'd say so."

"You got me. The old man wanted me to check in with you. Make sure you're unwinding."

Orla dragged herself out of bed and padded over silently to the window. The sun hung low in the sky, casting an incredible orange glow over the Gulf. Nature at her finest.

"So, you're not working?" he asked after a half minute of her not saying anything.

"I'm sure you know all about my evening," she peered out through the plate glass, checking left and right, habit rather than suspicion. "I'm sure you're watching me right now."

"Corinth. Bloody lovely place, I bet."

"It is."

"I've always wanted to visit Greece."

"Don't expect an invite."

"You trying to keep me away? Why would you... Oh... am I interrupting *something*?"

"Grow up, Jude," Orla said.

"Touchy. So what do you want me to say to the old man?"

Orla glanced at the man lying in her bed. "Tell him..." She hesitated. "Tell him, I'm content."

"Content?" A few seconds of silence filled the line. "As in *happy*?"

"I wouldn't go that far. Anything else I can do for you?"

"I think that's all he needs right now. He worries about you. You know how it is."

"I do. Bye Jude."

"Bye Orla." The line went dead.

Orla shut the phone and surveyed the bedroom. The place was a war-zone. Blankets lay rucked up at the end of the bed, cotton climbers holding onto the edge of the cliff for dear life. Bougainvillea flowers stained the tile floor, looking like a squashed tube of 80's hot pink lipstick. Orla's fingers went to her shoulder at the memory of Ares running into the wall while she straddled him, and the sudden pain of those spikey flowers and their thorns pressing into her back. It was a good memory.

She'd told Lethe that she was content, but what did that actually mean? Could finding one person, if only for a night and less than half a day beyond that help erase the branded deep pains of the past? The pessimist in her denied the possibility, but she wanted to hope. Just this once. Hope. And hope was a bastard. She didn't believe him when he said he was in love. You didn't fall in love at first sight. That kind of thing, if it existed, didn't get beyond lust. But there was something here, or could be, if she allowed herself to stand still long enough for it to catch up with her.

She sat on the edge of the bed.

Ares opened his eyes.

His gaze was unfocussed and vague, centered off on the middle distance until he smiled and turned his full attention to her. He pushed himself into a kneeling position and stretched. His pendant fell away from his chest. It was such a peculiar thing, a throwback to the Mediterranean men of the Seventies. It wasn't something she expected a thoroughly modern man to be found dead with hanging around his neck. And yet there it was. Maybe it was some sort of heirloom. Or he wore it for a bet.

"Good evening," Orla said.

"Is it?" He reached forward and kissed her on the forehead.

"The sun is setting."

"You know what that means?"

"What?"

"We missed another meal time."

"And work." She nodded to his closed laptop. "It looked important."

Ares sat back. He stared at her. "Can I ask you something?"

"*Another* question? Aren't you worried about losing the mystery?"

A slight frown crossed his handsome face. He didn't laugh. "Do you do this a lot?"

That stopped her. An edge entered her voice as she asked him, "Do what?" Even though she knew exactly what he meant. It was fine for men to rack up the numbers, trawl bars for random snatch, but it wasn't the done thing for a woman to play the game that way.

"Sleep with strangers?" he said, confirming that she'd read him just right.

"Does it matter if I do?"

"I don't sleep with every woman I meet," he said. "As to telling them that I love them?" He shook his head. "I don't want to be some extended one night stand. Look at you, how could I not want *more*?"

"What if I don't want more?"

"Then I won't say those words again. I'll go now."

"Ares, just shut up for a minute and try and be... *normal* about this," Orla tried to find the right words, ones that wouldn't have him limping out of there like a wounded bird. "You don't know me. You have no idea who I am. What I do. You have no idea. You can't love me. Not me. Because you don't *know* me. You know a woman who saved your arse in an alleyway. You know my body, how I respond to the touch, but you don't know my secret places. The places where I hide my truths. The things that make me *me*."

"Then show me those places. Make me understand who you are."

"It takes a lifetime, Ares, not a nighttime. And what if when you start to know me, when I tell you even a fraction of the unspeakable things I've tried to shut out, you don't like what you hear? What if you can't deal with it? Or worse think you need to fix me?"

He puzzled expression confirmed that he didn't understand. "What could be so *horrific* for you to fear it that much?"

"You don't want to know."

"I do."

"Believe me, you don't, not tonight. Maybe if you're still here tomorrow I'll tell you one truth, and if you're still here the day after I'll share another, and the day after another."

"I should like that."

"You won't, I promise."

"You underestimate me."

"Maybe. But why don't I tell you your first truth?"

"I am all ears."

"I really need a stiff drink and a decent meal."

"I am curious, has vodka always been your drink of choice?"

She smiled at that, the first time she'd smiled in a few minutes. "Recent habit," she said. "I blame my friend, Konstantin. He says once you drink it, it's in the blood."

"Your blood must be crystal clear if last night is anything to go by."

*

They browsed the windows of the shops along the narrow cobblestone streets on the way to a small restaurant that washed up against the edge of the beach. Outside, facing the blue waters of the Gulf, a large wooden gazebo was heavy with grape vines and tiny golden lights. It was very touristy, trying to catch magic in a cliché and sell it to the lovebirds.

"Now," Ares when they had been seated at their table and hard ordered a bottle of wine. "Tell me about yourself."

"Don't want to try a little warmer reading this time?"

"No. I'd like to hear it from you."

"Okay, you weren't wrong, I *am* strong. I believe in doing what's right, fiercely so. I enjoy good food and have few friends. I am a polymath. My specialty is languages. I am conversant in a dozen, several dead, and I'm a workaholic. That's about it."

"Hardly, I'm sure," he said, but he followed her lead. "I am driven. Head strong. Educated. And I have a soft spot for Frank Sinatra."

"I prefer Ella Fitzgerald."

"Ah, the Queen of Jazz. Incredible voice, I'll give you that, but she's no Blue Eyes. Now, tell me, what do you do when you're not on vacation?"

"I'm retired," she lied.

"Good for you," he said, not buying it for a moment. "I am an archeologist."

"A real life Indiana Jones?" Orla raised her wine glass to her lips. "Lucky me."

"It's the hat," he said. "That and I made my parents call me Indy when I was ten."

Orla laughed at that.

"They asked me what I wanted for my birthday. I could have had anything. I decided on the new name. They were not amused."

"But I am."

"Now for the quiz part of the evening," he said. "Have you heard of the Diolkos?"

If the sudden change of subject was meant to catch her off guard, it didn't. "It's the stone road they used to pull boats across the Isthmus centuries ago."

"Indeed it is, and it is a national treasure. Unfortunately, the government doesn't consider it particularly important, which believe me is a crying shame. They don't provide the help or funding we need to preserve our historic antiquities if they aren't somehow fashionable." He said the last word with so much contempt she almost choked on her vodka.

But it led to a better question, "If the government isn't funding your work, who is?"

"I'm heading up the dig for a private benefactor. It's not as impressive as it sounds. My mentor runs the show, but this is my chance to prove my worth." He unclasped the gold necklace and placed it into Orla's hand. "Do you know what this is?"

Orla ran a finger over the heavy pendant. She hadn't really looked at it beyond thinking of it in terms of *bling*. It was circular, gold and stamped with unusual symbols that slowly spiraled towards the centre of the circle.

Now she recognised it. "The Phaistos Disc," she said.

"It is identical to the original found on Crete, except smaller of course."

"Some say it's a hoax."

"People call things a hoax when they can't explain them."

He was right. She had first-hand knowledge, including discovering the Seal of Solomon, thought lost to all. It had cost her everything, including herself, but she had stopped a war between Israel and Palestine. But she couldn't tell Ares that.

"People like me have been working to decipher the symbols for a long time," he continued, "but it's not eager to give up its secrets, rather like you." He grinned at that. "One group believes it to be a genuine Minoan Religious Inscription, but there are still some markings that nobody has been able to decipher." He closed her hand around the necklace. "The amazing thing is, I believe this smaller version is a direct copy of the real original. The one in the Heraklion museum is itself also a copy, enlarged. The true original is yet to be found." He paused. "I want you to have this."

She shook her head. "I can't. This is solid gold. It must be worth a small fortune."

"A not so small one," he said. Rising from his seat, he moved around behind her and tenderly ran his fingers through her hair. "I had thought about diamond earrings, but you don't strike me as a diamond kind of woman," he said.

He fastened the clasp of the necklace and it nestled into place between her breasts, warm from his body. It was far more ostentatious than anything she might normally wear, and it was far more than she felt comfortable accepting.

When he returned to his seat, he rested his elbows on the table. "That disc represents the single passion of my career."

"You don't have... I don't need it."

"But I want you to have it, and it's mine to give. It will help you understand me, and that's what this is all about, isn't it? Knowing each other. This is my obsession."

She understood.

The waiter appeared again, delivering an enormous seafood platter lined with chips of ice, and a bottle of wine to replace the vodka.

By midnight, they had eaten their fill and the conversation had circled back on itself half a dozen times, often returning to old school music. Rising together, they linked arms and left. Instead of heading straight for the hotel, Ares directed her toward the pier. The walked along the wooden deck as the waves gently rocked the platform from side to side. He looked out across the dark waters, the lights from the bay shining on the waves like fireflies at dusk. Finally, he spoke.

"I love this country," he said. "I do. Truly. I love the weather and the culture. I love the history. Did you know that this is where they laid the Argo to rest?"

"The Argo?"

"Yes, it was here that the ship was consecrated to Poseidon and then taken up into the sky, or so the legend goes. All of their journeys had come to an end and they needed to pay homage to their God."

"Old gods and tall tales. What really happened to it, assuming there was ever a ship called the Argo?"

"Oh, there was," he said, with a confidence bordering on fanaticism. She recognised that edge to his voice.

"And you think they scuppered it here?"

He shook his head. "No. I think they moved it."

"And that's why you're digging for the Diolkos? The map you were looking at on your laptop – I thought it was a road of sorts, but it wasn't was it? It was a ship. You're searching for the Argo."

Finally, he smiled. "More precisely, we are searching for anything that might support our request for additional funding. Should we find the Argo, that would be wonderful, obviously, but there are many ships to excavate."

He had given nothing away.

"You are digging for proof of the Argonauts? They're just myths, stories to tell children at bedtime, like your old gods."

"One day, Orla, we will all be myths."

FIVE

Orla slipped the one piece bathing suit up her legs. Hooking her arms through the shoulder straps, she cinched the clip at her back and adjusted her breasts. Straightening in front of the full-length mirror, she took a good long look at herself.

She still wore Ares's pendant. The bright white suit and the burnished gold of the necklace stood out against her olive skin. Lightly spritzing her arms and legs with the fragrant oils, Orla worked her muscles until her skin shone.

She heard movement outside the bathroom.

"Ares?" She called, sliding open the frosted glass door.

Instead of Ares, she saw three men. It took her a fraction of a second to realise she recognised them, and a fraction more to place them.

Ares's attackers.

Her gun was in the drawer beside her bed.

She wasn't going to get to it before they tackled her.

She needed to improvise.

Orla moved fast, reacting before the intruders realised they were in danger. She charged at them. Snatching up a heavy glass ash tray from the table, she pitched it at the first man like a heavy baseball. It hit the mark, crushing his cheekbone.

Hands clutching at his face, his knees buckled and he went down.

The second figure, with his arm in a sling, held back. The last thing he wanted to do was engage and take another battering. He was the clever one. The last man launched himself at her.

Orla was ready for him.

She didn't slow down, meeting his charge head on.

Instead of cannoning into him bodily, she pivoted and rose, using the furniture to help her vault, her feet scaling his chest. She wrapped her legs around his neck and brought him down, crashing into the sofa. He pitched forwards, on top of her. As he went down, Orla twisted, gripping his hair as she forced his head back. There was a deep sonorous *snap* of a single bone breaking. It was more than enough.

The man didn't move.

The smart one, the guy with his arm in the sling, tried to run.

Orla launched herself at him, slamming his head into the edge of the door. As he went down, she stamped on his injured arm. He screamed, clawing at her bare legs, trying to push her away, but Orla was relentless. She delivered a rapid series of punishing blows, each one aimed at his damaged arm, and when that hung limply at his side, she worked over his ribs. She felt them crack. That didn't stop her. She drove her fist into his face, again and again and again, each punch faster, harder, than the last as he spat blood. He pissed himself. That didn't stop her. She didn't stop until she had beaten the life out of him. And even then she didn't stop for a good fifteen seconds, driven on by the fury of adrenalin as it coursed through her system.

She almost didn't hear it.

Instinct saved her.

She ducked and rolled away from the corpse as the serving tray whistled through the air towards where her head had been. It missed her by inches, bouncing off the door.

Orla snatched it up spun around, parrying a wild punch from the man with the busted-nose and the bruised forehead. She switched her grip, fastening her weaker hand onto his wrist and twisting the bones until she heard something inside snap, then with her stronger hand, she whipped the silver tray up under his chin, into his Adam's apple. The impact snapped his head back and left him gagging and reeling.

Orla hit him again; a fist to the temple. That rocked him. A second floored him.

Orla was on top of him in a heartbeat. She rammed the steel edge of the tray into the man's throat again, this time pushing down hard enough to do some serious damage.

"Who the fuck are you? Who sent you? What are you looking for here? Get the answers right and you might just walk out of here."

But he couldn't answer.

He couldn't get a word out, not while she cut off his air supply.

She relented, easing off the pressure on his throat.

"Speak," she demanded.

He didn't. Not at first. He struggled to suck down a breath. She waited.

When he finally mustered the will to speak, he spat, "Piss on you, whore."

"I only let my friends do that," Orla said.

He'd had his chance.

He died twitching like an epileptic.

33

She didn't feel any pity for his plight. She'd offered him a way out. His two friends hadn't had the same luxury. Orla stood up and surveyed her ruined hotel room. Three dead bodies and a tornado's worth of damage. The old man's credit card was going to take a pounding.

She heard movement in the corridor outside, followed by a tentative knock on the door. She retrieved her gun before she answered the knock. There was a chain. She didn't use it. If the newcomer wanted in, a piece of metal wasn't going to stop them unless it was bullet shaped. Nevertheless she opened the door just a crack to see who was there.

It was Ares.

"I heard..." he searched for the word. "A commotion?"

"It's fine. I dropped something. Three somethings to be precise."

"Clumsy," he said.

"Now you know something else about me," she said.

"Are you ready to go?"

"Just give me one second and I'll be right with you." She closed the door. Thinking fast, she hid the gun in a wall vent, picked up her sandals and her room key, and returned to the corridor outside.

"You sure everything's okay?"

"It's all good," she said. She couldn't tell he if knew she was lying. She concentrated on closing the door and getting away from the corpses. She scanned the corridor but marked nothing out of place. Nothing that didn't belong.

"My God, you're beautiful," he said.

She didn't answer.

He tried to kiss her, but she really wasn't in the mood.

"We need to talk," she said.

"Why don't I like the sound of that?"

34

"Those men who attacked you on the night we met, did you know them?"

"No."

"Are you sure about that? You hadn't seen them somewhere. Maybe recognise them from hanging out at the bar, at the dig? Seen them at the same café you normally drink at, or maybe they just keep walking past you in the grocery store?"

"I haven't seen them before," he insisted. "They were just petty criminals. The islands are full of them. Why do you ask?"

"I saw them again."

"When? Where? Are you okay?"

"I told you I'm fine. It's taken care of."

He didn't ask her what she meant by that.

Orla placed the Do Not Disturb sign on her door and followed Ares to the lifts.

*

The beach was awash with flesh of every shade of pink and red to golden brown, and every body shape and size from the brittle skinned praying mantis grannies who'd spent decades in the sun, to pot-bellied albino men, almost certainly Russian, in unflattering Speedos which left nothing—not even their religion—to the imagination.

Ares and Orla spread their blanket across the sand and settled down. He opened the small cooler he'd brought and retrieved two iced bottles of Perrier water.

"It's the third day straight you haven't been at work," she said. "Isn't someone going to miss you?"

"I took a few days off. They'll get by."

Doubt nagged at the back of her mind. She could accept that three men she'd killed in her hotel room had been opportunists when they attacked Ares the first time, but twice? No. It wasn't coincidence, it was a pattern. Ares was either an exceptionally talented liar, or he really was oblivious.

It bothered her.

*

The gentle waves swirled about them, cocooning them in a warm embrace as they entered the crystal waters. Ares coaxed Orla deeper until the waves buffeted their chests.

Water carried its own connotations. She could shower, bathe or wash her face without having flashbacks to being waterboarded or half-drowned in a bucket in a dingy basement.

The water here wasn't too deep. She still had her feet on sand.

But as they ventured deeper that changed. The sands shifted. The water came up to her chin.

"You don't have to do anything you don't want to do," Ares said, sensing her unease. "But, believe me, it is most beautiful beneath the surface, like you." He slid the mask over his eyes. "If you sink to your knees, you'll see what I mean." His voice was muffled as the mask covered his nose. He waited for her to make up her mind.

She could do this. It was no more threatening than the soaker tub in her hotel room. She pulled her mask over her face and swallowed a deep gulp of air. Sinking to her knees, Orla opened her eyes to the beauty rippling out before her. The clear turquoise waters stretched on and on like a lucid dream. The golden sands of the beach gave way to darker, volcanic rocks. Farther on, the navy blue darkness of the deep ocean lazed along the edges of the lighter waters. Many-coloured fish dotted the serene, underwater landscape and the occasional turret of reef reached to the honey-filled air just above the surface.

"It's beautiful, isn't it?" he said when they were standing again. He helped her find her footing and then pulling off his mask.

"Not sure that's the word I'd use," she said. "It doesn't do it justice."

"Treasures are regularly recovered here, most recently a substantial amount of temple pottery and old coinage, no doubt paid as sacrifice, has been found in this area. Once in a while, a brass statue creates a stir among the locals."

"And you keep what you find?" Orla asked. She knew how the world worked; it made little difference that the government was frugal with the purse strings, even when it came to the preservation of relics, they wouldn't be averse to rolling in the riches any such antiquities offered up.

"Scavenger laws," he said.

"In other words what they don't know won't hurt them?"

"You are a smart woman."

"I've been called worse," she said.

"Now let's see if I can find you a keepsake." Ares pulled the goggles back down over his eyes and kicked back, floating face up in the surf. "Coming?"

Orla shook her head. "I think I'm all swum out for now."

"Let me take you back to the beach then," he offered, treading the water.

"You promised to find me something. You can't do both. Now go, swim."

"Okay, I'm going to search that area near the pier. There are rich pickings to be had."

"I believe you. I think I'll have earrings to go with the chain."

37

"Yes ma'am," he twisted in the water and dove down, swimming the fifty odd feet to the pier. He covered the entire distance on a single breath.

Turning to the beach, Orla headed in. She wrung out her long hair as she waded to shore. She reached their towel, the sun-hot sand stinging her bare feet. She grabbed a fresh towel and dried her face.

She watched Ares in the distance, seeing him dive and surface, dive and surface, moving around the thick timber posts of the dock. Reaching for her sunglasses, Orla settled down, lying on her stomach with the wadded up towel for a pillow. The sun's warmth dried her skin quickly. She let herself relax. It wasn't easy to let go. There were three corpses in her room that were going to need to be dealt with, and a whole heap of questions she needed to unravel about just who she'd been sharing her bed with and why those people were so intent on robbing him.

Around her, sun worshippers slept. She envied them their ability to simply switch off the woes of the world. She had no such facility. In the silences horrors returned. Dark moments came alive even in the brightest sunlight. More than once in the last month she'd hallucinated the presence of the Beast on the streets of Warsaw. He'd been there. She would have sworn on her life. Of course, he hadn't been anywhere. He was in the dirt. Dead. She'd faced the Beast and overcome. It was too easy to relive those days, that cell, the piss-stained mattress and the fear, and forget the part where she'd saved herself. She hadn't waited for rescue. She'd faced her personal devil and banished him.

But the old man was right, damn him, she was still running from him, throwing herself into anything and everything as a way of not having to process things.

She wasn't one for therapy or talking through her feelings. She looked out across the water. Ares was nowhere to be seen.

She scanned the beach in case she'd missed him leave the water. The fat man hadn't moved since they had arrived. His skin resembled a rare steak, the bloat of his belly beyond any natural shade of pink. There was no sign of Ares on the sand.

She still wasn't worried.

Orla pushed herself up to give herself an angle to see the pier. He hadn't surfaced, or if he had, she'd missed it, which was more than possible. She looked back towards the hotel's balconies.

"He didn't come back," the fat man said, staring up at her.

A shiver of alarm rippled through her and the veneer of a nice picture postcard morning she'd painted over the events of the hotel room rinsed away like rain on a watercolour painting. She dropped the towel and started for the pier, moving fast. It wasn't far off, but with the sand shifting beneath her feet making it harder to run, it seemed miles away. She broke into an easy lope, light on her feet so her toes didn't sink into the shifting sands. She kept her eyes focussed on the area where she had last seen Ares surface. There was no sign of him.

She reached the thick pylons and paused at the edge of the water. The ridiculousness of it hit her then; it was a game. He was fucking with her. He had no idea about the dead men, or her past. She'd kept both from him. She scanned the beach and walkway.

"Ares?" she called out, her voice whipped away by the rush of the rolling tide.

Instinct kept her alive. Instinct was her best defense and instinct was clawing away at her core. She needed to trust her gut. Something was wrong. Instead of heading inland, she bolted into the water, the waves battling her movements, trying to force her back. She pushed, wading deeper and deeper as the surf surged and splashed up around her. Others swam on their backs looking up at the sun, splashing and playing games. Down the beach a group did water aerobics. They were all oblivious. She dived forward, throwing herself under the surface. The salty water and grains of sand stung her eyes. She blinked against them, ignoring the discomfort as she fought the current. Orla powered on, no longer pretending to be a weaker woman to flatter his male vanity; she swam against the undertow, kicking and moving with grace and power, breaking free of the pull. She couldn't breathe underwater, so rose, sucking in a deep lungful of air, and dove again. She hung in the azure blue water, scanning the sea bed. She knew what she was looking for, and didn't want to find it.

He floated near the bottom, his body at an odd angle, his head and arms pointed downward. She swam towards him, but couldn't get to him without rising for another breath. She went down again. She could hold a single breath for almost a minute and a half. Ninety seconds. That was long enough to realise that Ares was tied to the cement base of the pier.

She needed to rise again, but couldn't leave him like that. Water filled her mouth. It spilled down her throat. She had no choice but to arrow upwards towards the surface, and when she broke through into the air, she coughed up the salt water, purging her lungs.

As she fought to breathe, she waved her arms frantically, semaphoring the shore.

There was no point shouting, the distance and the joviality of the swimmers neutralised any chance her cries had of reaching the shore. She stayed above the waves as they bullied her back and forth.

Someone saw her. At first they waved back, then she saw someone coming running along the pier, launching herself into the water.

She landed beside Orla.

"Are you okay?" she asked as she surfaced.

"He's down there. Help me." Orla pointed into the water before diving again.

The twenty feet from the sun to where Ares was tied to the base of the pier's stanchion with ropes around his wrists might as well have been all the fathoms down to the deepest trench in the blackest water. The pressure built inside her. It was hard to hold onto that one breath so desperate to burst out of her lungs.

She reached him.

Orla wrestled with his hands, trying to pull him free of his bonds without looking at his beautiful face caught in the grimace of death. His sea green eyes were wide open. There were no bubbles of air rising from his parted lips.

Something tugged at Orla's arm. The woman. She pointed upwards. They needed air. At that moment, the last of Orla's breath leaked out through her pursed lips, replaced with a sharp pain in her empty lungs as her body craved one more breath.

She kicked out toward the surface.

She kept her eyes trained on the golden rays of the sun as black tendrils of unconsciousness swirled in the corners of her vision.

Someone pushed her from below, propelling her the last few feet to the surface.

Orla threw up seawater as she desperately struggled to swallow down breath after agonizing breath. She fought to grab another lungful of air before diving again, but the woman grabbed her arm.

"You can't," she yelled. "It's too deep. The only thing that happens if you dive again is this time or the next you don't come back up. You can't help him. You saw the ropes. We have to call the police."

The other would-be rescuers reached them.

They helped her ashore.

Her chest and throat raw with the sting of seawater, Orla dropped to her knees when she reached the sand, fresh waves rolling in around her as she battled with the reality that more death had followed her to this little Greek paradise.

"Can I call someone for you?"

Orla looked up at the woman.

"I can call someone?" she repeated, her French accent thick.

Orla shook her head.

"There is no one? For him? He has no family?"

"I don't know them."

The crowd had alerted a policeman who arrived on the beach, breathless. The French woman waited with Orla while she answered his questions. Not that she had answers. None she could give.

Was this on her?

Was this payback for Poland?

No, she reasoned. Thinking like that, self-flagellation, was indulgent. It wasn't on her. She'd rescued him from a beating, then killed the men when they came back looking for him. This wasn't about her at all. It was all about him.

And again she was left wondering just who her Greek lover had been.

Had. Such a horrible change of tense.

The rest of the day swam by in a flurry of sounds and movement. Questions, endless questions. She was escorted to the police station. She sat in the interview room alone. The return of her demons was barbaric. This quiet restorative, a few days by the sea to forget, to heal, threatened to consume her. The anger she felt inside was about so much more than Ares. It went all the way back to Poland, to Israel and beyond. She needed to compartmentalise. To block it out. She answered every one of their questions as best she could. The problem was she knew so very little about him. She didn't care what they thought about her. She wanted to help, but didn't have the answers, not even to the simple things like where he lived, how old he was, who he worked for, friends, family. None of them. Did he have any enemies? She had to bite back on the urge to ask, considering the fact he'd been tied to a pier in the middle of the ocean and left to drown, what did *they* think? Part of Orla realised she would never escape the cage of her past and her job because that was who she was. She wasn't like other people. Trouble followed her.

That fact, had they known it, would have been enough to terrify his killers, but it would have told them exactly what was going to happen next.

"You should go back to your hotel and get some rest," the police officer told her. If only he knew what was waiting for her in the room, she thought bitterly. "If we need you we will be in touch. Needless to say, we would request that you stay in the country for now."

"I'm not going anywhere," she said.

A taxi waited at the curb and she clambered into the plastic back seat and told the driver the name of her hotel.

She paid him and went inside, trying to decide what to do to make three bodies disappear.

She opened the door and went inside.

Her room was a mess; worse than when she'd left it. It had been ransacked. But that wasn't what she was processing, not yet. Someone had removed the bodies.

Whoever had done this was long gone.

Her first instinct was to check the vent where her gun, her phone and her various passports were hidden. They were still in place. The room's safe had been forced open, but the currency she'd stashed inside was still there, meaning nothing had been stolen. Of course it hadn't been a *burglar* – it had been a cleanup team. Either sent to finish the job so fatally botched by the three dead men, or someone sent to mop up after them.

"Who *were* you?" she said to the empty bed.

She dialled the number automatically. It was always her first instinct with things went south.

"You know the old man said try not to kill anyone while I was here?"

"Should I be worried?" Jude Lethe asked.

"You tell me. I've racked up four corpses so far."

"Jesus."

"No, he was already dead long before I got here." Her voice sounded like it belonged to someone else. She couldn't feel anything.

"What's going on Orla?"

So she told him. About the mugging. About the dead men and how her room had been cleaned up, then trashed sans corpses, and about the man she'd been sleeping with ending up tied to the foot of the pier.

"I don't even know where to begin," Jude said.

"I'm not coming home before you even suggest it."

"I wouldn't dream of it."

"Good. I'm going to get some answers."

"You know I'm here if you need me. Are *you* all right?"

She considered his question. "I'm not sure," was the best she could manage. Not so long ago she'd been content. That was the curse of her life, of who she was. She had allowed herself to think that for just a few hours she might get away with being normal.

She hung up.

The mobile rang again.

She let it go to voicemail.

SIX

Morning rose like heartburn, the sun's rays creeping up the sides of the buildings in red hot agony. The heat seared gold circles into the backs of Orla's eyes and she rolled away, trying to escape it. Eventually, she rose from the jumbled mess of blankets.

She baulked at her reflection in the mirror. She contemplated returning to bed, but one look at the side where he had lain was enough to remind her of who she was, and what it meant to be her.

She ran to the shower.

Cold water ran down her back, bouncing off her buttocks and splashing the shower wall. She held her hair against her chest and allowed the streams to chase down her body. Leaning her head back, she shuddered as the water clung to her scalp, cooling her too quickly. She reached for the control and turned it, feeding heat into the cold stream. Her skin accepted the warmth.

Turning off the flow, she wrapped herself in a towel.

Her day was essentially mapped out for her: *solve the riddle of Ares.* She had to find out the basics first, who he worked for, his family background, the circles he moved in when he wasn't hooking up with tourists, they all came together in the pattern that would eventually unravel the *why* behind his murder.

Most of the things they'd talked about were still vivid in her mind, like their conversation on the dock about the Argo being laid to rest right here in Corinth. That might be something or nothing, but right now it was a fragment, something to move beyond. And then there were the initials on the paperwork he'd been studying when she moved up behind him: *AI.* Were they anything beyond the obvious reference to artificial intelligence?

She dressed in a loose white V-neck blouse and a long yellow skirt, complete with golden hieroglyphics sewn across the hem. She ran a brush through her hair and slipped on her sandals. She still looked like hell, but at least now it was a freshly scrubbed hell.

The sun had risen quickly, covering the city of Corinth in a blanket of warmth. The heat radiated off the walls of the buildings.

"*Geia sou sexi!*" A young man in a dirty tank top and cut off shorts called out as he looked backwards on his tiny bicycle, appreciating the view before disappearing down the lane.

Rounding the corner of the hotel, she heard a sharp cry from above. Not far beyond the rooftops, a lone hawk glided on the breeze. Close enough to differentiate the various hues of brown adorning its feathers, it battled the winds as if buffeted by the waves of the ocean, its feathers ruffled as it adjusted altitude. It cried out again; its voice shrill and lonesome –calling for its mate. It hovered for a brief moment before dipping sharply and diving away.

Orla crossed the road to the railing edging the beach and watched the hawk disappear. She rested against the metal rail. The choppy waters of the gulf were highlighted in white as the wind stirred the eddies. The waves rolled in.

Adjusting her sunglasses, she scanned the beach.

A woman in a hideous neon yellow one-piece battled an umbrella as she attempted to stab it into the sand. Her friend shouted orders for her to face the thing into the wind so it wouldn't turn inside out. Normally, it would have made Orla laugh, but she was in no mood for levity.

A thin man caught her attention, wearing a white bucket hat and open-toed sandals. The black messenger bag he carried slipped and he pushed the strap further up his shoulder before kicking at the surf. Allowing the waves to spray his knees, he reached down and picked something up. Wiping it against his shirt, he seemed to notice he was being watched. Shielding his eyes from the sun, he focussed on Orla and then waved.

Orla pushed away from the metal railing. "What the hell are you doing here?"

Grinning widely as he neared, Jude Lethe held out his arms as if presenting himself to an adoring crowd. "I'm on vacation. Like you. I was going to ask you to pick me up at the airport, but you turned your mobile off."

"This isn't a game," she said.

"Four people dead seldom is. Besides, I figured you'd need to see a friendly face, not just a friendly voice for once."

"You didn't have to."

"That's where you're wrong. The old man would have castrated me if I'd stayed home." He grinned.

Instead of berating him any further, she sighed. "They murdered him, Jude."

Jude's dropped his bag and pulled Orla into an embrace. The breeze gusted for a moment and Orla's hair wrapped about his face, and for just a moment they were united.

"I've got you," he said, which would have been amusing at any other moment, but after what he'd been through in Peru little more than a month ago, and his pledge to never leave Nonesuch again, was anything but. It was love. The kind of love she could understand. The unquestioning bond of someone who would and did risk their life for you again and again, willingly, in the knowledge that you would be there for them every single time of asking. They were family.

"That's never going to happen again," she said, pulling away.

"I know," he said. "I'm not trying to shrink you, but maybe Frosty told you about Peru. I lost someone. I've got an inkling what you're going through. I want to help. It was different. I mean, she was ordered to get close to me, but ..." He trailed off.

"I know," she said. And she did.

"Thanks." He gestured towards her hotel, changing the subject. "I'm staying at the Club Hotel Casino down the beach a bit. Want to hitch a ride so we can check in?"

"We?"

"I booked the Imperial Suite on the old man's dime, I figured you might appreciate a change of scene."

"*Imperial* suite?"

"Don't worry. A little luxury never hurt anyone, and I promise I'm not a threat to your virtue."

His answer was so ludicrous it made her smile, despite everything, but her mind was already fully engaged in work mode. "Jude?" she asked. "You can pull satellite images from your laptop, can't you?"

"Yep Why?"

Orla turned without answering and walked towards her hotel.

Jude hurried to keep up with her as she reached the road.

She briefed him as they walked. Just the facts. Meeting Ares, the work he was doing, his mentor running the site, and the necklace, the leather-bound book and ultimately the three muggers who she knew for certain had targetted him. She started to feel connected to her own thoughts again. Alive. Orla Nyrén was no passenger. She made her own destiny, and that destiny was to find the person responsible for Ares' murder and extract a price. Passion and fire grew inside her as she talked. She seized upon them.

Jude waited downstairs while she went back to her room for the last time. It took her five minutes to chuck everything into her suitcase, retrieve her gun and open the door to leave. She hesitated in the doorway, scanning the room to be sure she hadn't missed anything, any clue that might help her. Sometimes the clues were in what *wasn't* there, not always in what was present. She tried to recall what was missing: the laptop and his notebook. There was no sign of his bag, but she couldn't remember if he'd taken the items to his place when he'd gone back for a change of clothes, or if he'd left them on the marble table.

She left a decent tip for the cleaning staff. They were going to earn every Euro of it and then some. Once she closed the door that part of her life was over. The card they had on file was a one shot arrangement, the name and the passport that secured it, bogus. Nothing about the woman who had lived in this room was real. Nothing could be linked back to her. She was about to disappear. It was what she always did.

SEVEN

"Not bad." Jude dumped his messenger bag on the couch and palmed a tip to the bellhop. "I could get used to this." He made his way to the floor-length windows and opened his arms to the stunning panorama.

"You make it sound as though the Manor is a fleapit," she said. She held her hand over her eyes, shielding them from the bright light that stretched itself around Lethe's slight frame. The suite was more like a luxury apartment – the glass doors opened directly onto a private stretch of the beach and an exclusive pool. The bedrooms were on the opposite sides of the living space with a main lounge area, dining and kitchen. It was beyond opulent, it was ridiculous.

"The old man's going to hate you when his bill comes in," Orla said.

Jude turned away from the view. "It'll go straight to the accountant and be filed away under operational expenses. Thank Her Majesty. Not that she ever thanks us." He paused for a moment. "You hungry? Should we go out?"

"No. Or rather yes, I *am* hungry, but we've got things to do we can only do from in here, so, room service?"

"All work and no play, eh?" Jude nodded knowingly. "Right, you order, I'll set up. I need lobster, Coke and chips."

"Lobster? For lunch?"

"King for a day," he said with a grin.

Orla dialled zero for room service and twenty minutes later a grand lunch of steak and salad accompanied by lobster with a side serving of fries arrived. She poured herself a glass of wine.

Orla settled into the couch next to Jude and watched him work.

Jude Lethe was a genius. Noah always said he was the most dangerous man he knew, simply because he could bankrupt the world without leaving his bed, never mind the other stuff he was capable of. The thought of him ever going dark, that there might be an Anti-Lethe out there, didn't bear dwelling on. He was indispensable. Orla watched as his tracking system pinpointed them, complete with a layout of their room. It took him less than sixty seconds to identify them as heat sources. The image delay was significantly less than she'd expected given the signal was bouncing up to the satellite and back down to his laptop and being processed as raw data along the way.

"So, mission objective?"

"The blueprints on Ares's laptop had an insignia on them. It was a circle around the letters AI."

"AI? Like Artificial Intelligence?"

"Same letters, but I suspect a very different meaning, but don't let me sway you. Dig." She grabbed a piece of paper and pencilled the initials. "We're looking for anyone with a grudge against him. Anyone who wanted him dead or stood to gain from his death. You know the deal. The kind of stuff you do for the old man when he says 'find out everything you can'."

"I know the deal," he said.

"Potentially AI could be the initials of the dig's mysterious benefactor."

"Or his own," Lethe said, "What do you know about him? Last name? Address?"

"Fuck it."

"Fuckit? That doesn't sound very Greek.".

"I don't know anything about him. Not even his last name." She wracked her brain for what she *did* know. "Diolkos."

"What's that when it's at home?"

"An archeological dig on the Diolkos. It's where he said they were excavating. There aren't going to be many digs along that site."

"Then we've got him. Hold on. Here we go," he said thirty seconds later. "Ares Petridis."

"Petridis?"

"Jesus, your boy was loaded. Old money. His family owns an international import business."

Orla leaned forward. "Where are they based?"

"Here." Lethe angled the laptop so she could see the screen. Reaching for his plate, he ate a couple of cold fries. "No reference to AI though."

"The diagrams were of a ship," she said. "But he said their goal was to uncover the Diolkos. Stay with me here, but what if they really have found the Argo?"

Jude frowned skeptically. "*The* Argo? As in Jason and the Golden Fleece? Not being funny, but why would anyone be looking for a mythological ship? It's a bit ridiculous."

"About as ridiculous as Caesar's sword or the Seal of Solomon," Orla said. "And someone told me not so long ago everything's eventually going to become a myth."

"If his family's in shipping, chances are we're talking a bottomless pit of money. These shipping magnates are seriously wealthy, top one percent of the one percenters.

53

Okay, let's think. If the A in AI is Argo... then what? Argo Incorporated?"

He pounded on the keys to run the search. "It's a knitting company."

"It is not!" She laughed, grateful for the absurd distraction.

"Look for yourself." Three old ladies smiled back from the screen. "I don't think this is it."

"They look like the Grey Sisters with their one eye and one tooth between them," she said. "Argo Incentive? Invention? Industries?"

"No, no, and no." Jude sighed. "Anything else you can think of?"

She was about to say no, frustrated, as she kneaded her neck, her fingers tangling with the gold chain. She fished it from underneath her shirt. The disc caught the sunlight and seemed to shine with an inner fire.

"This."

Jude reached for the golden disc and leaned forward, his eyes narrowing as he attempted to read the script. "Okay, what is it? I assume it's *something*?"

"It's a copy of the Phaistos Disc."

"Okay," he turned the disc over several times. "There are inscriptions on both sides."

"An ancient Minoan religious poem."

"You said he had a book?"

"It was a leather journal."

"Did you get a look at it?"

"No. I saw it once and that was it."

"So how do you know he was looking for the Argo?"

"I don't."

Jude reached for his drink. "Okay, let's try attacking this a different way. What's so special about the Argo? Why would someone want to find it?" He turned his attention back to the laptop. After tapping away for a few seconds, he read aloud. "The Argo was a ship named after Argus, the ship builder. In Greek mythology, Jason and the Argonauts sailed safely to many locations with the Argo. Blah, blah, blah... okay, here we go, according to the legend, the Goddess Athena placed a magical timber into the prow of the ship – one that could render prophecies."

"There's no such thing as magic," Orla said.

"Oh come on. Who wouldn't want to find a splinter of wood that would tell you the future? It'd be like a sliver of the true cross. Can you imagine how much that'd go for?"

"Pull up the satellite overview of the Diolkos and let's zero in on the dig. If we can work out what it is they're actually digging up, maybe we can figure out what they're really up to."

The hunt did not last long.

Lethe's rig was able to route the entire Diolkos system running along the canal that was cut in the 1800s. Made from stone, much of the road remained buried, but it was easy to track the length of the old portage road. In addition to pulling the image of the Diolkos, two road bridges and two submersible bridges were as obvious as the Isthmus itself.

"What's that?" Orla pointed at a line at the west end of the canal.

"A military bridge," Jude pinched and zoomed on the touchscreen and the image grew. "It looks old. Almost certainly not in regular use."

"Where's the dig?"

He moved the screen again. "Right here." The images grew larger and moments later, the rectangular shape of the sectioned off area near the canal was full screen.

"I want to know who's funding it," she said.

"There's no mention on any of the filed permits, but someone knows. Money has a way of tangling people up in red tape talk."

"Jude?" she began, her tone different. He looked at her and waited. She took in his kind face, the battered innocence behind his eyes. He'd seen some things, and not behind the safety of his computer screens. He was on his way to broken, just like the rest of them, and Orla didn't want that for him. It wasn't right.

Finally she said, "I never thanked you for saving my life."

"Which time?"

"Funny guy."

"If you mean Poland, that was all Konstantin."

She raised her hand to silence him. "And if it wasn't for you, he never would have known where I was. He wouldn't have found me. You're the one that watches us from the skies. You're the one that keeps us safe. I know none of us say it, but we all think it. So, I'm saying it, thank you for always being there."

"Shut up," he said, looking away.

Lethe didn't have real family, as far as she knew, but his pseudo-family was a bunch of emotionally damaged killers working in a covert team led by an old man.

"Okay, Disney-moment over. I need to *do* something," she said, standing up. "I'm going to go stir crazy in here."

"What do you have in mind?"

"A field trip."

"I don't do well in the field."

"I'll look after you," she said.

"That's what Noah said."

EIGHT

Orla was annoyed with herself.

It was good to have something *mundane* to be frustrated with.

Lethe had insisted on staying at the hotel, assuring her he'd be of more use monitoring her remotely and providing operational back-up as per Nonesuch. She let him hide. She knew it was all about Peru. No one acknowledged what combat was really like, not for someone like Lethe.

She wore her red dress and an earbud from which came the sounds of munching and chewing.

"Can you at least mute the mic when you're eating?"

"Huh?" he said.

"You're making me hungry."

"Oh, sorry." Jude cleared his throat dramatically. "Good evening, Miss Nyrén, I'll be your eye-in-the-sky tech support this evening. If you'll just take a moment to acquaint yourself with your surroundings you will see that there are exits to the front and rear, and several windows that could be used at a push, should madam require a stealthier approach."

"I'll just walk up to the front door," she said. "Not that there's actually a door. It's in the middle of nowhere."

It didn't take long for her to be noticed.

All the men stopped to stare. She let them. Mounds of dirt and grid maps littered the area. She walked down the slope carefully towards them. Even so, she nearly lost a shoe as it sunk into a patch of mud. The men were soaked with sweat and smeared with dust. They were in tee shirts and rolled up sleeves, or shirtless. They stopped what they were doing to watch her negotiate a route around the pits they'd excavated.

"Can I help you?" a deep voice growled beside her.

Orla turned gracefully, a wide smile on her face.

She faced a tall, muscular man dressed in, of all things, white trousers and an Easter blue long sleeved shirt. His apple red braces bowed about his giant pectoral muscles. Security ala Miami Vice, she thought.

"Can I help you?" he repeated, taking a step toward her. "Are you the new contact, Yvonne?"

Orla flashed him a killer smile. "That I am," Orla lied, smoothly.

"You're late. Mr Meyer is waiting for you. He's in a foul temper. He really doesn't like being forced to hang around in the heat all day." He attempted to smile but his face, unused to pleasantries, grimaced instead.

"Sorry about that, couldn't be helped," Orla purred. "Sorry, how rude of me, you know my name and I don't know yours?"

"Enzo," he said. He motioned for her to follow him.

"Italian? I didn't know they made them so big," Orla said. She really wasn't particularly strong on the whole gentle flirting thing. Enzo didn't answer. Jude on the other hand mocked her mercilessly via the earbud.

"That's all you've got? I mean seriously, you pretty much might as well have said, hey big boy, come up and see me sometime..."

Orla ignored his commentary and focussed on the Korth revolver sticking out from the back of Enzo's waistband. It was an extremely rare gun, and it was highly unlikely that a grunt hired as muscle for a dig would be able to afford the piece. Aside from that, the most obvious alarm bell of a question was why would he need a gun at all? Open carry wasn't permitted here. Maybe he had a permit, but it was unlikely he'd have one as security for an archeological excavation. Two and two wasn't making four right now. She hated when that happened.

"Mr. Enzo?"

He turned. "Just Enzo."

"Enzo, can I just say what a *beautiful* gun that is you're carrying. A Korth, if I'm not mistaken?"

This time, the man grinned. "She's my *belle*," he said enthusiastically.

"It's not a Bellezza, is it?"

He pulled it from behind and held it up for her to see, confirming that it was, indeed, a Korth Bellezza. "Beautiful, no? You know guns? I think you must, which makes you both beautiful and smart – a potent mix, Yvonne. I like that very much."

"You charmer," she said.

Enzo tucked the gun safely behind his back. He led her to a canvas tent on the far side of the site. Inside, the wealth on display took her by surprise. The rugs, the decorations, all of it, were incredibly lavish, like something from the grand old days of Hollywood.

Enzo pointed to a leather wing-backed chair.

Orla sat.

Enzo positioned himself just outside the tent.

She waited. Time passed slowly. Orla shifted uncomfortably. She was a sitting duck. She waited some more. Nothing. Finally she mumbled a question to Jude. "What's going on?"

"Nothing. Looks like everyone's off site except for your babysitter. Maybe they've gone for lunch."

"Perfect. I'm not loving this," she added and uncrossed her legs to stand. "Anything on this Yvonne person I'm supposed to be?"

"Not yet. A surname would be handy."

"Sure, I'll just go up to the boss and say in my culture we always address strangers by their full name, you first... that ought to do it."

"Yeah, yeah. Sarcasm really doesn't suit you... Oh, here we go."

The tent flaps opened to reveal a wheezing, corpulent man. He wore a formal, starched suit. Sweat poured from underneath the brim of his hat and ran down the sides of his face. He drank greedily from a glass of iced water before addressing her with a thick German accent.

"I'm sorry to leave you waiting like this, Miss Baudin, please forgive the rudeness. I was unexpectedly detained. Of course, compared to your own delay my forty five minutes is nothing. We have been waiting for you for two days. I assume you have a very good reason?"

Orla hesitated, shifting the ruffle of her dress lightly with her fingers. "I apologise," she said, hoping it would suffice.

"Yvonne – may call you that?" He didn't wait for her answer. "I didn't expect you to be so young and... attractive – I admit to finding it distracting. I had expected a frankly more dowdy specimen, especially given the extent of your work. I can only assume you have no interest in dirt and decay, but rather that AI sent you here for some..." He paused, struggling with the challenges of the vocabulary. "*Purpose?*"

Orla stood and approached him. He watched her with hungry eyes. "Of course," Orla lied, "There is always a purpose."

He waddled toward her and reached out to touch her cheek with fat fingers. Orla allowed him the brief moment of intimacy. She didn't flinch, or fend him off. Not this time. Memories fought their way to the surface: the Beast had touched her like that. It was a way of owning her. She resisted the urge to vomit.

"And you are –?" She searched for the name, which danced tantalizingly right on the edge of memory, fighting the Beast to be heard. "Mr *Meyer?*"

"The very same"

She offered her hand. "It is very much a pleasure to meet you."

"Oh that pleasure is all mine," he took her hand in his and squeezed it gently. The gesture was again far too intimate for a stranger.

Orla withdrew her hand.

"German name?" he asked. She shook her head.

"French."

"Really? Yvonne is of Germanic descent, no?"

"Indeed, but Baudin is as French as names go."

"I think you'll find that it is in fact also Germanic, my dear. It means 'brave'." He turned away. "Unfortunately, so many are brave but also foolish." Reaching the desk, he sank down into his chair and leaned back heavily. "So tell me, why have AI sent you to me, Miss Baudin?"

Orla thought quickly. "For a situation report, obviously."

"Were they unhappy with my recent communique?" he asked, reaching for more water.

"You and I both know that things are seldom so straight forward when money becomes such an important factor."

"Indeed, but we are in the fortunate position of no longer needing further funding," He ran his hand over the various items on his desk, coming to rest on a brown leather book. She recognised it. Ares' journal. Her heart skipped but she showed no pause at the sight of it.

"I've never come across a case of someone refusing free money."

"Money is never free. You must understand that money is not our aim here: as the saying goes, it is the root of all evil. Besides, there is one thing people crave more than money."

He stood, easing himself closer to Orla, with little regard for her personal space.

"Power," Orla said.

"Always," he agreed.

Orla eased away from the fat man. "So how do you intend to have one without the other?"

Instead of answering, he sat back down. She'd failed whatever test he'd laid out for her. "You're wasting my time. Tell AI we will continue as planned. Enzo!" He called. The tall man pushed aside the tent flap. "Escort this woman off site."

"Sir." Enzo gently took hold of Orla's elbow. Rather than fight him, she allowed him to take her out of the tent and escort her to the edge of the perimeter road.

"Please do not return," he warned her. "There is no place for a woman like you near to such danger."

He left her there and marched back to the tent.

"You there?" Orla asked when he was out of earshot.

The voice of Jude started up in her ear. "Always. Everything okay?"

"I'm fine. I didn't get much. I'm going to have to go back." There was silence on the other end. "They have his journal. They either took it from my room, or his home. But either way, it confirms they're behind his murder. So I want to see what's in it that's so important."

"Okay, but we need to do this properly, no charging in blindly. Come on home."

"Right." Orla began the walk back to town.

*

"I'm fine!" Orla insisted, tossing her sandals aside. "I'm just," she searched for the words, "a little rusty." She sidestepped him and headed for her room.

He followed her. "You can't be rusty. You get rusty, you die."

"Right."

His words cut her deeply, but he was right. She turned away and opened the door to her room. "I need some time. Alone."

"Take all the time you need," Jude said, not unkindly. "I'm going for a swim."

A swim. Such an innocent activity, but not any more. "Please don't," she said, memories of Ares drifting underwater, lifeless eyes staring at her, still fresh.

Jude was right. You get emotional, you lose your touch: you die.

She'd been incredibly lucky that Meyer had thought she was their contact, doubly so that he'd given her a name to work with. If he'd known the truth, she would probably be back in chains and rotting on a foul fluid-drenched mattress waiting to die again.

The memory made her skin crawl.

It was time to remember who she was.

She closed her eyes.

She focussed on her breathing.

Inhaled.

Every caress, all of his stupid promises, every shared moment – breathed out, sent away. Banished.

When she opened her eyes, she was herself again.

She was Orla Nyrén.

She was an operative. An agent. A killer.

NINE

The funeral of Ares Petridis was well attended.

The tiny church by the beach was crammed with well-wishers and, Orla assumed, family members. The service was entirely in Greek. She loitered at the back, feeling like an intruder on so much personal grief. She was the last person to talk to Ares on the day he died. In some circles that made her an obvious candidate for his murder. She didn't feel like putting herself forward for interrogation.

The bright morning sun sliced through the building's narrow windows creating an otherworldly aura within the church. Orla avoided looking at the coffin. It was on a bier at the front, by the altar. Instead she focussed on the congregation. Plenty were in silent tears. She showed no outward signs of mourning. She was here to observe, to find out more about the people connected to Ares, to get a candid look at those who loved him and those who did not.

She scanned their faces for any hint that a mourner was hiding something.

The only person she recognised in the entire congregation was Enzo.

He was so physically imposing he was instantly recognisable, even from behind.

When the service drew to a close, Orla's attention centred on one woman who stood out from the rest. Light radiated about her thin figure. She spoke quietly with another mourner. Even though she was clearly an older lady, she was a vision of grace and poise. A powerful woman in so many ways that had nothing to do with physical strength. She was tall, in six inch heels, the woman's figure defined by a black dress that looked like melted licorice poured over her body. The dress was long sleeved, with a slight vee in the neckline and edged the bottom of her knees with a 1930's flair. She clasped a black Hermes purse in her left hand and brushed her dark brown hair away from her face with her right. She was elegant in a Sophia Loren type of way. Lethe's comment about old money rang true. She saw Orla through the crowd and to her surprise, the woman came over.

"You must be Orla?"

"I am," she said carefully. "I'm afraid I don't know who you are."

"Oh, I think you do, my dear," the woman said. She gave a brief nod to a man trying to attract her attention from across the nave. "Ares was my son," she said, her gaze settling on the necklace. "I see my son gave you his prized possession?" She smiled ever-so-briefly. "So typical of him. He wouldn't have given that to God Himself, but he hands it over to a strange woman to impress her."

"I'm so terribly sorry for your loss," Orla said. Wearing the necklace, on balance, might have been a mistake.

The woman ignored her sentiment. "Tell me, did you love my son?"

"We hardly knew each other."

"That's not what I asked you, is it?"

"What do you want me to say? You want me to say that he was the love of my life?"

"If it is the truth."

"I liked him," she said.

"Then I am also sorry for your loss." She extended her bejeweled hand. "Maria Petridis. Ares was my only child." The handshake was tentative, almost skittish. "My son was incredibly gifted," she continued. "He never divulged the intricacies of his work, obviously, but he often dropped hints, like breadcrumbs that could be followed if something ever happened to him. I warned him so many times that his work might get him killed."

"I don't understand. He was an archeologist."

"He was a Petridis first. We come from a long line of ancestors dating back to the time of the ancient heroes. Our family has always done well. There is a legend that affects all of the families in this area, perhaps he told you?"

"We didn't talk much," Orla said, then regretted the obvious callousness of the statement and how the woman would surely take it.

"Two lines: one hailing from Theseus and one from Jason."

Recalling her conversation with Ares the night before he was killed, Orla asked, "Jason? As in the Argonauts? The Golden Fleece? That Jason?"

Maria snorted. It was the least ladylike sound Orla could imagine coming from such a demure frame. "That man was no hero; he was an adulterer, a kidnapper and a murderer. He doomed his descendants. It was the Gods' will. "

"Let me guess, your family is descended from Theseus?"

Maria smiled. "Indeed it is. Naturally there is a fierce rivalry between the families. As they say, there are two sides to every story. What they often neglect to say is that one is always right."

"Or three," Orla added, causing Maria to raise an eyebrow. "Hercules? No?" She leaned forward in her chair. "He was their best friend. Who better to tell their stories to the world?"

Maria broke into a grin. "You are quite intelligent. It is no wonder Ares loved you."

"It really wasn't love, I'm sorry. I know it makes for a better story, for a bond between us, but it wasn't love. It was the beginning of something, maybe. It might have become more than it was, but love? That's not something that happens over a matter of days."

"He was convinced that you were his reward, my dear, so believe me, from his side it was very real."

Silence fell between them.

Orla broke it. "If you want the necklace back, you can have it."

Maria dismissed the idea with a wave of her hand. "No, no. It's yours. That is not why I came to talk to you. I wanted to give you his notes."

"His notes?"

Maria retrieved a package from her expensive purse. She rubbed her thumbs over the smooth surface before handing it to Orla. "Photocopies," she explained. "He didn't know I made them. Nearly every page from his journal. You'll need this to help you find his killer. I trust you will find answers in here when you find the questions you need to be asking."

Opening the envelope, Orla took out a small sheaf of papers. Each page was covered with hand drawn hieroglyphics and translations - codes that deciphered ancient languages only known to a handful of people.

She decided against revealing that she'd seen the original journal on Meyer's desk.

"What happened to the original?" she asked.

"Stolen. Someone broke into Ares's house and took his journal and laptop. Nothing else was taken as far as I can tell." She put a hand on Orla's and gazed deeply into her eyes. "I believe you can find out who killed my son."

"Why would you think I can?"

"Because it is what you do." The statement was delivered as absolute matter-of-fact. "I know you helped him fight off those robbers, or should I say you fought off those robbers without his help. I know that you carry a gun. But more importantly, despite spending a lot of money looking for answers, I don't actually know who you are, Ms Nyrén, and that confirms it for me.

"I want my son's killer brought to justice. I don't mean in some court of law. I want genuine justice. An eye for his beautiful eyes. He was destined for great things and now..." Her dark eyes were wet. She looked away, causing one tear to tumble down her cheek. "I don't know if you have children, but..." Her voice caught and she paused before finishing her sentence. "I was terribly hardened before Ares arrived." The look she gave Orla was desperately sad. "He softened me. He was my light, and now he's gone and my world is cast in darkness."

Orla resisted the urge to reach out and take her hand.

"Please, find out who killed my son." Despite the please it was more a command than a request. Orla got the distinct impression that Maria was used to getting her way.

"I will," Orla promised.

"It was a pleasure to meet you." Maria stood, tucking the handkerchief into her sleeve. "I trust we shall do so again, at least once more."

Orla nodded her agreement.

She reached into her purse and pulled out a small piece of paper. "This is my number when you are ready with answers." She smiled briefly. "Until then goodbye, Miss Nyrén, and good hunting." She maneuvered gracefully from the church.

Orla waited until she was gone and she was sure no one else was listening.

"You got all that?"

Jude responded at once. "Get those pages back here, I'll take a few of those Kourabiedes biscuit thingies, I've always wanted to try them."

"They only sell those at Christmas."

"You're resourceful, Orla. And don't forget the coffee. A guy could die of thirst in here."

"You've got room service."

"They brought me this thick treacle stuff."

"It's called Greek Coffee."

"Whatever it is, I don't like it. Bring me the caffeine of John the Baptist."

"You're a very, very strange man."

*

Jude pulled the curtains closed and then eased himself onto the couch next to Orla. "So, we start with the journal. I don't know anything about dead languages, that's your domain. What do you want me to do while you're reading?"

"Not sure yet," she admitted. She flipped through the photocopies. Every inch of every page was filled with Ares's tight scrawl. One sheet included a list of website addresses. She handed that one to Jude.

He fired up his computer.

Orla leafed through the remaining pages looking for some familiar symbols, anything she could trace back to languages she'd studied, or even had a cursory familiarity with. "Meyer mentioned AI. That's two for two. See if you can find any link between those sites and those letters." Frustrated, she turned over the next page. More meaningless scrawls. "I don't recognise any of this stuff."

"Orla?" Lethe turned his laptop so she could see. Again, three old women were captured on the image.

"We've done the knitting company conquers the world gag," she said.

"I know. But this isn't that AI." Jude pointed to the initials in the top left hand of the screen.

"Doesn't necessarily mean anything," he said. "Could just as easily some sort of weird obsession. They're old women, who knows how they think?" He tabbed through a few links on the site, turning up an exceptionally tenuous link. "They're based in Germany. Meyer is German. He kept insisting to you that Baudin was of Germanic origin. What are we looking at? Some sort of Aryan ideal? What do we actually know about Ares Petridis?"

"That his mother loved him very much."

"Which isn't exactly news to 99.9% of the civilised world."

"You'd be surprised," Orla said. She got up and walked across to the terrace doors. "Something about what she said bothers me. It was all about finding the murderer, not once did she ask me to find out *why* he was murdered."

"She's Greek. Maybe she's used to tragedy? Or maybe she only wants revenge. In her place I'm not sure what I'd think or say. She's grieving. You talked to her at her only child's funeral. She's hardly going to be thinking straight."

"Normally I'd agree, but she seemed very much in control."

"So what, she already knows the reason he died?" Jude let that sink in for a second. "She said his work might get him killed, and now it seems it did."

Orla nodded. "That's what I'm thinking."

He turned back to the screen. "Okay, so let's do this another way. We know Maria Petridis owns a shipping company." He started typing. "Maria..." Jude began humming the song from *West Side Story*. "Co-owns the company actually, with her husband, Khristos Petridis."

She hadn't seen an obvious father of the deceased at the funeral.

"What's the name?"

"Kephas International, or KI. They ship worldwide, but most of it is centered here in the Mediterranean. Give me a second and I'll pull up their routes."

Orla scanned more of the photocopied pages and finally found a few familiar markings: some symbols from Ares's necklace.

She put the object on the table beside the drawings on the page to compare them.

"Okay, that's peculiar," Jude mused.

"What is?"

"There's a route that ends nowhere."

"Nowhere?"

"It just stops. It travels toward Egypt and then stops short of the coast."

He was right, the route tailed off before it reached the shore. "Some sort of software glitch?"

"Maybe. Or maybe it's going to an offshore platform. An oil rig or something? The end point isn't far from Alexandria. You'd think it would terminate in a major city."

She realised what Ares was doing with the disc. He was trying to decipher the final markings, which meant he obviously believed there was more information hidden in plain sight. He just couldn't make sense of it. "It's not a language," she said, confusing Lethe.

"No, it's a city."

"No, listen to this," she read a section of Ares's notes aloud. "Brother turned on brother and they immersed that which could destroy them. The unspeakable was silenced, the unthinkable left inconceivable and that which was possible was rendered unattainable and removed from the hands of man."

"The unspeakable was silenced," Orla repeated.

"And the unthinkable. Neither sounds particularly appealing."

"Just the kind of stuff a relic hunter would love to chase."

"Sinking the Argo would count as rendering it unattainable and removed."

Orla shook her head. "It wasn't sunk, it was raised into the sky to become a constellation... because of the possibility of something terrible happening."

"And it was permanently removed from the hands of man." Jude clicked his ballpoint pen as he pondered. "Okay, it's a good story, but that's all it is. Let's not chase fairy tales. There's no such thing as magical timbers that can tell the future, even if they believed it back then. We're in different times. We've got to assume that if this is what we're really talking about, then it's about money."

"Meyer isn't interested in money. He wants power."

"Okay, so what kind of power can a bunch of old timbers give him?"

"If we assume they can't tell the future that doesn't mean they can't tell him something else."

The two of them sat lost in thought for a moment, then Lethe started typing, fast. He was chasing an idea. He entered another of the websites from the list. A large picture of a golden coin appeared on the right hand side of the search engine page.

"What's that?" Orla asked.

"A Ptolemaic coin," Jude said. "He clicked on the link and read out loud, 'Ptolemaic coins were used in trade between the Egyptians and the Greeks. Many have been located at old shipping routes including Thonis.'"

"And that shipping route ended near Alexandria?"

"Thonis," Jude continued, "also known as Heracleion, housed the site of celebration known as the "Mysteries of Osiris" that was observed during the month of Khoiak."

"Heracleion is Greek and Thonis is Egyptian, but they mean the same thing. They're the same city. It was only rediscovered a few years back. An entire city lying under thirty metres of water, lost for centuries. There's all sorts of treasures and statues, gold and coins and old pottery. Enormous statues of the Gods half-buried and pieces of gold lying in glittering piles on the sea floor."

"So KI are shipping to and from Heracleion?"

"Looks like."

Orla rubbed her face with her hands and watched Jude connect the dots.

"Let's review," he suggested. "One: Ares was looking for the Argo. I'm willing to bet he found it. Two: he knew what the markings on the Phaistos Disc meant." He glanced at Orla before continuing. "Three: he told you about Jason and the Argonauts, Hercules...who were on the Argo together..."

"And Maria made sure I knew the story of the two feuding family lines."

"Four: Meyer stole the original journal to help him find the ship."

"But why kill him over a book?"

"People have been killed for less."

"Wait, they already know where the ship is. Ares was involved in the dig. Hmm."

Orla flicked through until she reached the end of the journal copies. She was searching for the blueprint she'd seen on Ares' computer. She found it, but it wasn't an exact copy. Rather it was a hastily scrawled outline of a boat on the very last page of the photocopied journal, suggesting it was one of the last pieces of the puzzle the dead man had discovered

"If they have unearthed the Argo," Orla said, "we have to assume they have access to those timbers. Which means whatever power they believe the timbers have is in their hands, or very soon will be. Magic or no magic."

"So we help ourselves to the timbers," Jude suggested. "Make ourselves targets. They come after us."

"And we'll be ready for them."

"The only problem is we don't actually know what we're looking for, other than a few old bits of wood."

"Maybe not, but we know where to look," Orla pushed the last page across the table. Lethe looked at the crude outline of the ship and the bold X had been drawn near the prow. "We're going back to the dig site. Tonight."

"What's all this 'we' business?" Jude said.

"Fine," said Orla. "I'm going back."

TEN

So much for the cover of darkness, Orla thought. The entire area was lit up with a deep golden glow. A bank of floodlights made sure there was nowhere to hide. She studied the site from cover. A lot had changed in the short time she had been away. 'Yvonne's' visit had obviously put the wind up Meyer. The German had doubled down on security.

"There's triple the manpower down there now," Jude said in her ear. "Easily. You must have really ruffled some feathers. Your best approach is from the west, loop around behind them to come up from the beach side."

"That works. Meyer's tent is that side. I want to see if there are any missing annotations in the photocopies we've got."

One of Meyer's goons passed close by her hiding place.

Orla unsheathed a knife. "They're not military," it was an easy observation to make. "They're muscle for show."

"Don't get cocky, kid," Jude said. His Harrison Ford impression was miserable, but he was right. Underestimating the enemy combatants was a sure fire way to go home in a box.

She broke cover, keeping low as she approached the guard.

He was tall and appeared to be wearing fatigues. One kick to his kidneys was all it took to lay him out. Orla slit the man's throat. She didn't even think twice about it. Her fourth kill since landing on the island. Some holiday…

She grabbed the man's hands and attempted to drag him behind the boulders to get him out of sight. She could barely move him. She grunted. "Jesus."

Jude laughed in her ear. "He's been eating his porridge. Okay you're good. No more hot spots in the vicinity. Move out."

A tarpaulin had been bundled up and abandoned beside a pile of dirt a few feet away. Staying out of the brightest pools of light, Orla scrambled across the dry ground to retrieve it and took it back to the body. Weighting it down with a few bricks, she did her best to cover up the evidence.

She moved closer to Meyer's tent.

She listened for movement. Any hint of motion.

"You're good," Lethe said.

She stayed on target, moving from cover to cover in an erratic pattern to remain unseen as the hired guns made their circuits.

Orla reached the tent.

She could make out the shadows of several people cast against the canvas. Another steroid-muscled man stood guard at the drawn tent flaps. She moved around the back, careful where she placed her feet. The chatter inside grew louder. She crouched, listening.

"I don't like it. We've got no way of knowing what sort of shit they'll rain down on us if we deviate from the plan."

Meyer's voice was easily distinguishable. "Irrelevant. You think too small. All of this is just another step towards our possession of the artifact. That is all that matters. That will change everything."

"It doesn't, it simply paints a target on our backs. This is bigger than any of us."

"I will agree that it is bigger than AI could have anticipated."

Hearing the mention of the familiar acronym, Orla placed the edge of the knife against the fabric and opened a small slit, giving her a partial view of the inside. Three men stood around a pit that had been dug in the ground. Meyer faced off with two others - one a short, white-haired man with round pebble glasses. The other, a spiderish bald man with black goatee. He clasped his hands together in supplication, putting himself between his two stouter companions.

"They won't brook desertion or any change of plans, Adler," the small man with glasses said.

Adler Meyer sighed extravagantly. Orla saw him reach into his coat pocket. "I am so very, very tired of your preaching. Do you lack the conviction to see this through?"

"I—"

"You know your fate."

"Please," the man with the goatee pleaded, trying to place himself between the other two. "Let's not be too hasty."

"Hasty?" Pebble Glasses wheeled on him. "Everything you do is timid. You are a mouse, Siegfried. Grow a pair. Don't let Adler bully you into being his bitch."

"I can see where you stand," Meyer said coldly.

"I am trying to get you to see reason," Pebble Glasses said.

"Reason?" Meyer chuckled. "The reasonable answer would be to agree to the new plan."

The little man straightened, attempting to make himself taller. "I don't think so."

"Luckily, it does not matter what you think. As ever the majority rules."

"No," the man objected.

"I said the majority rules," Meyer repeated.

The gunshot was shocking, even with the silencer on. Meyer put the put the pistol back in his pocket. "And then there were two. I take it you have no objections to the new plan, Siegfried?"

"What have you, done?"

"I did what was necessary. He could never see the bigger picture. *We* are different, aren't we?"

Siegfried mumbled something incoherent.

"Aren't we?"

A tremulous agreement was muttered.

Meyer smirked. "Enzo!" he called. The giant entered the tent a moment later. "There's a sack of shit here that needs dumping in the latrine."

"Sir."

"And do something for me, Enzo."

"Sir?" The big Italian was a man of few words.

"Make sure the assistant hurries up. We don't want this exposed for any longer than necessary."

Enzo hoisted the dead man over his shoulders. A trickle of blood dripped down the dead man's face before it fell from the end of his nose. All this was lost on Meyer.

"You have grown soft, Siegfried. When we started this journey, you had the balls of a colossus."

With that, the fat man turned on his heel and followed Enzo out of the tent.

Siegfried sighed loudly, raking his hands down the sides of his face, like he was trying to peel a mask away. Squatting beside the hole, he started mumbling. Orla strained to make sense of his words, but they were incomprehensible. Finally, he stood up and left the tent.

Orla widened the tear quickly and slipped inside.

"I'm in," she moved straight to the desk. The journal was still where she'd seen it earlier, on top of a pile of papers, sitting in plain sight.

"Incoming," Lethe said in her ear.

She thumbed through the journal.

She didn't see anything that wasn't already part of the photocopies.

She saw the *opposite*.

The last page with the X marking the location of the supposedly "magic" timbers had been torn out.

"Out. Now!"

Orla put the journal back on the desk and slipped out through the small tear. She heard others enter as she left into the cool night air.

Keeping low, she moved away at pace, running fast, keeping low, arms and legs pumping furiously as she closed the distance between her and the main tents over the dig site. She was exposed for seventeen seconds. No shouts went up.

Ducking under the fabric she remained crouched, surveying the dig.

The ship itself, though it wasn't obviously a ship, wasn't completely uncovered, but the excavation was well under way. Sections were exposed in the various open pits around the site. It covered a huge area. From where she crouched, little of the visible structure appeared analogous with any part of a ship. Outside, the waves rolled in, the crash against the shore a constant soundtrack. At the far end of the site, towards the stern, she noted a group of workers using shovels to dig a fresh pit. Because of the X on Ares's sketch Orla was more interested in the bow. She moved quietly towards what she hoped was the front of the vessel.

If that page had been torn out of the journal before Meyer stole the book it made sense that his people didn't know where to look, but it also begged the question who tore that page out? Ares himself? Someone else?

She reached the larger pit at the bow-end of the site. The workers had dug down to the prow of a ship. The exposed timbers were charred, and appeared brittle to the point that simple contact could cause them to crumble to dust. The excavation work must have been painstaking, brushing away layer upon layer of dry dirt to slowly expose the treasure hidden within the earth. Any wrong move and the whole thing could collapse in on itself like so much sand to be carried away by the beach breeze.

How was she supposed find the right timbers? She couldn't exactly dig for them, even with the X on the map to lead her to the right area. And even if she stumbled upon the right timber, the exact perfect one that she was looking for, it would certainly be in such a state of disrepair, it was almost certainly beyond her ability to salvage.

She lowered herself into the pit, being careful not to touch the exposed timbers. The last thing she wanted to do was trigger even the slightest disintegration.

It was cramped down here, and the pit filled with deep shadows beyond the rim because it was out of the glare of the floodlights. Avoiding touching the ship altogether was impossible. She placed a hand on it to steady herself on the uneven ground.

A warm, tingling sensation ran through her fingers and chased down her arm.

She pulled away instinctively.

She reached out tentatively to touch it again, thinking about the reality of what her fingertips rested on: a relic of antiquity that hadn't seen the light of day for thousands of years.

"You're looking for a piece of wood that has the same markings as the disc," Jude said in her ear.

"Maybe. Maybe not," Orla whispered.

She inspected the wood closer, praying that the markings – if there were any – would still be decipherable. It was beyond a slim hope; the wood was simply too decrepit to make out any sort of detail or scoring. She had no choice but to use her hands to try to wipe away the thin patina of earth and debris that clung to each broken beam in the pit. Some of the timbers were still held in place as part of the bow, others lay on the ground where they'd crumbled away from the main structure.

She attempted to lift one of the smaller pieces, only to find it fused to the one underneath.

"This is ridiculous," she rasped, aware that her voice would carry. She sat back on her haunches. "The wood's burnt beyond recognition. It's fused together. I don't have anything to pry the timbers apart. Even if I did, I don't have enough time."

"You can only do what you can."

"This is ridiculous... If this really is the Argo... Jesus, Jude... what am I doing here?" Orla stood slowly in the confined space. There was nowhere to hide if Meyer and his goons came looking. As she turned on the spot, she saw a large bucket with various digging tools including a trowel.

She eased the tip of the trowel between two beams of wood and tried to pry it free, just opening a couple of millimetres of breathing space for her to work with.

It was like trying to pry apart a boulder.

Orla tried again, this time, wedging it with more force, putting her weight behind it. She heard a sharp *crack* and a small fragment of calcified wood rolled to the ground, it was more like a lump of stone than the sliver of wood she'd expected.

She ran her fingers along the surface of the charred wood, noting the various ridges and grooves commonplace in logs. Kneeling in the dirt, she continued to feel out the timbers, not sure what she was hoping to find. She held her breath. There had to be something – anything – to hint at what was so precious – and potentially *powerful* – about this relic.

There was nothing.

She clawed at the wood with her nails, frustrated, then dug down into the muck encasing the prow, scooping out more dirt to expose more and gradually more of the rotten timbers. It took five minutes to clear away almost a foot of fresh beams. Five more to clear away the dirt from over the thick foremost beam of the ship. There was no obvious decoration or carving.

"There's *got* to be something," she said, her voice thick with frustration.

But of course there didn't have to be *anything*.

Ten minutes became twenty. On her hands and knees, she scratched around the exposed timbers frantically working where the team had already dug; she cut deep into the layer of dirt as the prow bowed gently down and into the soil beside it. Beads of sweat broke out on her forehead, dripping into her eyes as she scrabbled away at it, clearing the dirt away in a rush.

She paused to wipe the sting of sweat away with the back of her hand.

"Clock's ticking."

"Not helping, Jude. I'm not a fucking archeologist. I haven't got a clue what I'm doing here."

"Okay, well, there's no serious movement in the compound, so I guess you're good for a while, but you don't want to be there all night."

She drove the tip of the trowel against the base of the hole, working it hard until flecks of the coffee-coloured rich earth wept out of it; a puff of dust billowed up into her face.

Orla dug furiously at it, using her hands to pull free more of the soil until she was able to reach into the hole in the side of the timber and feel around on the inside of the wood. It was cold to the touch, the soil wet and thick with the odours of salt and decay. She lay on the ground, her face pressed against the ship's prow, her arm buried in the hole up to her shoulder. She might as well have been reaching blindly into Hades itself for all the good it did.

"There's *nothing*," she said, conceding defeat.

"Time to get out then. Live to fight another day."

Orla ran her hand along the curve of the prow one last time as she withdrew her arm carefully from the hole. Her fingers grazed up against something, the faintest indentations, two of them, parallel notches a few inches apart, like something had been inset there.

"Wait a second, I think I've got something," she whispered, hardly daring to hope. She lowered herself back down until she lay flat on her stomach and could reach all the way into the hole unimpeded. She ran her hand up and down the inside of the ship's prow as best she could, feeling out every grain and crease with her fingernails in an arc of maybe six feet until she found what she was looking for: a seam that ran the length between the notches, matched on the other side by identical partners.

"We've got movement coming your way."

"Meyer?" Orla asked.

She slid her nails into the seam and heaved at it.

"Probably Enzo, given the heat signature. It's one big mofo."

The wood didn't give an inch. Pulling harder only earned the sudden searing pain as her fingernail bent back close to the quick.

Orla pulled herself from the hole and reached for the trowel.

"There's definitely something here," she said, sliding the tip of her trowel along the seam. The triangular point disappeared into the impression. She worked the blade back and forth, conscious of the vandalism she was perpetrating as an entire section of charred wood tore free in a cloud of charcoal dust.

A length of wood maybe half a metre long fell at her feet. Like all of the exposed timbers it was badly charred. She picked it up and turned it over in her hands. Something caught her eye, tiny patch near the splintered end – it looked fresh, no sign of burn damage. It was hard to be sure in the near-dark, but she'd certainly found *something*.

She was out of time.

She stashed the piece of wood in the backpack she'd brought in with her, then launched herself upwards. Her hands gripped the edge of the pit. Gritting her teeth, she hauled herself out, shoes scrabbling at the walls as she climbed.

"Move!" Jude yelled in her ear.

Once out of the pit, she stayed in a crouch, controlling her breathing and staying silent. She couldn't risk a word, not before she got a fix on the guard.

She couldn't see him.

Then she heard a cough right behind her and she froze.

She craned her neck, half-turning.

A guard stood just beyond the tent wall, on the other side of the fabric.

There were millimetres between her and discovery, the thickness of a sheet of canvas the only thing preventing him from staring straight at her.

She didn't dare move.

Physics dictated that the floodlights would cast her shadow against the tent, meaning if she moved he'd see her like shadow play.

She started as a sudden flare illuminated the wall of the tent, bringing the silhouette of a man's face into sharp relief on the canvas wall for the briefest of moments as he lit a cigarette. He drew in a deep breath, the match burning out. His shadow disappeared. Orla's heart hammered against her breastbone. She still didn't move.

Move, she willed with the full force of her mind.

She wasn't telekinetic. She couldn't just push him away with her thoughts.

"Get out of there, woman," came Jude's urgent demand.

She couldn't answer him.

She couldn't move.

Orla scanned rest of the tent's interior. The other workers were gone. There was no one else in there with her. She couldn't risk rising, despite the numbness spreading through her thighs. The cigarette-smoking guard swayed back and forth, humming a nonsense tune.

He wasn't going to move on until he'd smoked the whole fucking thing.

All she could do was wait.

And wait.

Until finally the guard moved away.

Orla stood up slowly, working the blood flow back into her muscles before she crept along the canvas wall to roughly where she'd entered. If the easiest way in was West, the logical easiest way out was back East along the same track, which meant going past Meyer's tent again.

She whispered, "I need a route out."

"I guessed," Jude replied. "They're moving around constantly, but you're clear to Meyer's tent."

Orla rolled out beneath the canvas wall. She stayed low, looking, evaluating her next move. All senses primed. On edge. Expecting the worst. She made four more hired hands walking the perimeter. She'd never reach the car without them spotting her. Not walking straight out of there.

She made four more on the other side.

There were probably twice that she couldn't see.

Meyer had assembled a small private army for himself.

Orla launched herself from a crouch into a dead run. Sprinting flat out, not caring about the noise or the sudden flurry of movement. She reached Meyer's tent, skirting around it in an attempt to retrace her steps. She had her eyes on the prize. Less than a minute and she'd be out of there with whatever it was she'd pulled from the wreckage.

"You've got company," said Jude.

She didn't hesitate.

Breaking away from the tent she took off as fast as she could. Faster, her feet threatening to tangle. She heard leaden footsteps behind her as he ran her down. She was the racehorse and he was the shire – his two steps matched her four. She was a fast runner, but this guy had *momentum*, an unstoppable juggernaut.

She wouldn't make it. There was no way out. She would have to stop him and that meant body number five, because she couldn't risk trying to disable him.

Orla pulled her Jericho 941 and turned to shoot.

"Bellissima!" her pursuer cried, holding up his hands as he rumbled to a stop.

Enzo towered over her, a smile upon his face.

"Enzo?" Orla said, frowning. Why wasn't he going for a weapon?

"Yes." He lowered his hands, a smile on his face. "You came for an unofficial visit?"

"I..." Orla hesitated, unsure what to say.

"You shouldn't come here again. Meyer would not like it."

"I don't plan to."

"Good, because if you do come again, I will have to kill you." His face grew serious. "Don't *want* to kill you, Yvonne. That would be such a waste of perfect skin."

"The men you work for, who *are* they?"

"I can't tell you."

"Don't make me shoot you, Enzo. Just give me a name. Something."

"You are going to kill *me*?"

"Not if I don't have to. I'm not a murderer. I'm a killer. There's a difference. Tell me this: why do you work for them?"

"The pay is good."

"And that's it? Money?"

"I need to eat."

They heard a shout, either the discovery of the dead guard or the tear in Meyer's tent. Either way it didn't matter. She had to get out of there.

"You should go now."

"You're not going to try to stop me?"

"Why would I do that?" He smiled. "Goodbye, *Bellissima*." He turned and jogged off in the direction of the commotion.

The encounter was bizarre, but she wasn't going to waste the chance she'd been given. She holstered her gun and continued running, not stopping until she was out on the main road where Jude had a car waiting for her.

"Don't look back."

Orla reached the waiting cab and opened the door. She threw herself into the back seat, and slammed the door. She only said one word to the driver, "Go." He didn't need telling twice. He turned on the radio and a teenage singer wailed endlessly all the way back to the hotel.

She'd risked her life for a lump of charcoal.

She could only hope it was worth it.

ELEVEN

They stared at the chunk of blackened wood on the table between them.

Orla could tell that Jude was wrestling with the need to make some sort of wisecrack. The way he chewed on the inside of his lip was a dead giveaway.

It was that tiny sliver of untouched wood that fascinated Orla, and convinced her that this prize was worth the risk she'd taken. Somehow, for some reason, that tiny fragment, that splinter, hadn't burned.

"I think I've spotted the flaw in your plan," Jude said.

"Go on," Orla said, still staring at the relic on the table.

"You wanted to steal something the killer would come after." She nodded. "You wanted to prove who the killer was by using it as bait." She nodded again. "The problem is, nobody knows we have it."

He was right, of course. They knew that someone had broken into the dig site, that they had killed a guard, but the journal wasn't taken, nothing else was stolen. Meyer would have no idea that the artifact they were so desperately searching for had been snatched from under their noses, quite simply because they didn't know where it was in the first place.

"Meyer is behind the murder," she said. "He knew Ares was close to finding the timbers. I'm absolutely sure of it, and judging by the argument I overheard, I don't think he'd have been up for whatever Meyer has planned for them."

"Killing him was a bit extreme."

"Meyer's found the Argo, there was no reason to keep Ares alive. Meyer and his friends were arguing about a bigger plan dependent on the possession of the artifact."

"The timbers?"

She shook her head. "I don't think so. Not any more. I did. But something in what Meyer said makes me think this is just a step towards finding something of greater value."

Jude stared at the charred wood again. "Maybe we should ask it? It's supposed to tell the future, right?"

"Don't be ridiculous."

Orla picked up the timbers and examined the thin seam of untouched wood. There was something there, she realised, etched into the grain. Small points, flaws, seemingly random but not natural.

She took the Phaistos Disc from around her neck and turned it over in her fingers several times, looking for a similarity in the flaws.

She saw something, or at least thought she did. She needed Jude to confirm it.

"Look at this." She pointed to the image of a flower carved into one of the many sections on the edge of the disc.

"What am I looking for?"

"Look at the timbers, the small fragment that's not charred."

He did, going back and forth between the two artifacts.

"Holy crap," Jude said. "You're right, it's the same symbol. You can only see a couple of the petals, but you're absolutely right."

"There would have been more, beneath the charcoal."

"We need a CT scanner," Lethe said. "Something that can see beneath the layer of charcoal, if there's anything there to be seen."

"CT scanner? So a hospital then?"

"I'm thinking the Archaeological Museum of Athens. Remember that ancient Greek analogue computer, the Antikythera Mechanism?"

Orla laughed, remembering the similar machine unearthed by a doomed archaeological team on a small French island, which had led her and Noah on an interesting visit to Dubai. "I'm familiar with it," she said with heavy sarcasm.

"Oh, yeah, of course. Anyway, the museum brought in a CT scanner to get detailed images of the inner workings of the box."

"You think that scanner will be easier to configure for timbers than a medical scanner?"

"Yeah it should already be set up for artifacts. Less heavily used too. Museums don't have a lot of emergencies."

"Athens it is then."

TWELVE

Gaining entry to the National Archaeological Museum of Athens presented a different sort of challenge to entering the dig site. There were cameras, alarms and security guards. Which was to say, it presented little in the way of a challenge to Jude Lethe.

They entered through a loading dock at the rear, avoiding the parkland out front. The museum itself was set back in its own grounds from the main road, easily big enough to fill a couple of city blocks.

They had arrived in Athens four hours earlier.

Over a hasty meal, again on room service, Jude had quietly opened a backdoor into the museum's security system. He talked Orla through it, explaining that typically it only needed three steps to open a place up. First, find a regular user of the system, a cleaner or curator, someone particularly low on the paygrade who isn't too concerned when it comes to account security. His brute force algorithms made short work of the poor schlub who'd set his password as *Athens82* and he was in. Stage two was a little more complicated, the equivalent of digital sleight of hand. He set about fooling the security systems into giving the hijacked account every network privilege available. Stage three was all about covering his tracks. It was pointless getting in if everyone could see what you'd done, so this, he assured her, was the real art of the con.

Now, with the clock ticking relentlessly towards two in the morning, the pair of them hurried through a dimly lit service corridor. Jude used a tablet device to disable cameras as they passed by.

"Maybe we can re-appropriate the Antikythera Mechanism while we're here," he joked.

"Let's not," Orla replied, taking him seriously.

"I could," he said. "The most valuable exhibits are secured by individual security systems entirely independent of building security and monitored 24-7, but if you know what you're doing, it's just a challenge, and you know what I'm like with challenges."

"I do. And I repeat, let's not."

"You take all the fun out of life, Orla. You know that, right?"

They approached the service lift.

Jude held up a hand in warning.

They flattened themselves against the wall, listening. Both wore black, but that wouldn't hide them from the eyes of the approaching security guard if he was unlucky enough to take the wrong turn and head their way.

Orla tensed, centred, calm. She was ready to take him down as quietly as possible. She counted out his footsteps as they echoed in the cramped confines of the corridor, following them closer and closer until it seemed inevitable their paths would abruptly cross. She moved instinctively for the Jericho beneath her arm, not to shoot, simply to neutralise. One swift blow to the right pressure point and he'd go down. If he didn't, the second would disable him. Death against disability might not have been the worst option all things considered.

94

The footfalls stopped, ten feet away from their position. They heard a door open, a quiet greeting between colleagues and the soft closing of the door behind him.

Lucky guy, Orla thought. She was moving immediately, Jude two steps behind her. They had to pass the door to reach the lift, it couldn't be helped. Of course the guards' office had a window in the wall and a smaller one in the door itself, but they were just obstacles to be negotiated.

Orla paused at the edge of the door's inset window.

She peered through. Two guards, a man and a woman, laughed over something on a screen she couldn't see. Probably some YouTube video of cats or skateboarders doing pratfalls. Numerous screens in a bank behind them rotated through the various chambers and displays within the museum. Neither guard looked their way, nevertheless Orla ducked down low enough to creep beneath the window and moved swiftly on.

Jude wasn't quite so elegant about it, but he didn't trigger any alarms which was all that mattered.

The two of them made it to the lifts. Jude was about to summon one when Orla grabbed his hand and pulled him to the side. She drew him through a crash door and into the concrete stairwell that serviced the building in case of emergencies. It was orange-lit.

"Lifts make noise. We don't use them unless we have to. Last thing we need is a chime going off and some poor sod opening the door to see who's coming." Her voice echoed harshly in the cavernous stairwell.

"I get it," Jude said. "Bad habit. Consider it expunged from my muscle memory. No more elevators." He held out the tablet. "Right, the CT is three floors down."

"Any security we need to worry about?"

"The usual. It shouldn't be on regular patrols. None of the artefacts down there are on display and the rooms are alarmed. They're not going to be watching the scanner. It's not as if someone can just walk out with it, and who the fuck breaks into a museum to use a CT scanner?"

"Us," Orla said.

"That's because we're special," he said with a grin.

They descended the stairs.

They emerged in another white-painted corridor. She could see multiple closed doors. Again, Jude triggered a few command line prompts on the tablet to disable the cameras before they rushed on towards the lab housing the scanner. The joys of the modern world revolved around everything being online, every system accessible to those who knew what they were doing, even the keypads that served as door locks. Jude overrode the keycode and the lock disengaged.

They went in.

Closing the door plunged them into darkness.

They lit their Maglites, revealing the familiar donut ring of the CT scanner standing on the far side of the room. The platform used to feed objects into the scanner array had been adapted from its original bed for medical patients to a series of trolleys that could be swapped in and out as needed. She ran her beam over the trolleys; there were no artefacts, but a toolbench to one side contained an array of implements presumably used to prepare the objects for scanning.

Jude powered up the machine while Orla removed the timber from her pack.

She placed the charred object carefully on a trolley and wheeled it into position by the scanner. Some of the edges had splintered and a large fissure had opened up, threatening to split the piece of wood in two.

The tray atop the trolley was on a slider that extended into the donut hole.

"You work here, I'll be outside making sure nobody comes calling."

He nodded. "I'm here if you need me." He tapped a finger against his ear.

She nodded, taking the tablet, and left the room.

Proper strip lighting illuminated the corridor, meaning precious few shadows and places to hide. She crouched down out of the range of the nearest camera. She didn't know how Lethe killed the cameras, so her plan was simply to avoid them.

She glanced at the tablet. It couldn't track the movements of the guards – they were too far underground for satellite imagery to be useful, and it wasn't equipped with thermal imagery or anything like that. What it could tell her was if any alarms were tripped, giving them a head's up before the fecal matter exploded all over the antiquarian fan.

She noticed a flashing light and an alert that the main door had been breached.

They hadn't come in that way. That meant more visitors. The museum was popular tonight.

She slipped back into the CT lab, closing the door behind her.

"We've got company. The main door alarm's pinging. How long do you need?"

"Ten minutes."

"Can you do two?"

"No."

"Okay, we'll have to improvise. I'll buy you ten minutes, but after that we're out of here. I'll be back for you."

Orla returned to the corridor and sprinted for the stairs, not caring if the cameras saw her this time. The guards were going to have their hands full with the new burglars. The coincidence of the double break in didn't sit well with her. She took the stairs two at a time, only slowing when she reached the main exhibit level.

She drew her Jericho and opened the door.

It was too quiet considering a break-in was in progress. She couldn't make out any signs of disturbance except for the steady beeping of the alarm coming from the security office in the distance. She edged out into the corridor, scanned left and right for hostiles, then moved rapidly, closing the distance to the office in a few seconds. It was empty. She went inside.

She cycled through security camera views until she saw what she was looking for—the last thing she wanted to see—a body lying in the entrance hall. The dead man wore a guard's uniform.

She double checked the floorplan on Jude's tablet, stowed the device in her backpack and headed out of the office.

As she moved she spoke to Jude. "We've got a guard down in the entrance hall. I'm coming back to you. We need to get out of here."

"That's nowhere near ten minutes. I need time. Even when the scan's done I've got to copy it across or the whole visit's pointless. You promised me ten minutes."

"That was before the dead bodies started showing up."

"Doesn't change anything. I still need at least seven more minutes."

As she reached the lift she sensed *something* out beyond the range of sight at the far end of the corridor, a ripple in the shadows, and ducked.

Pure instinct.

The bullet took a chunk out of the wall where her head had been.

She threw herself back and away, twisting as she slammed into the concrete floor. She used her body's natural momentum to roll away. It was all about making herself as difficult a target as possible.

She scrambled to her feet, running in a half-crouch, until she reached the far wall, the Jericho out in front. The stairs were twenty feet behind her. She couldn't get a visual on the gunman. There were plenty of side rooms for them to avail themselves of.

Six and a half minutes.

Dare she risk going for the stairs?

She decided against it, staying flat against the wall.

The shooter stepped into plain sight and unloaded his rifle in her direction.

He was firing blind.

Orla held her position.

The bullets pitted the wall behind her, one after the other. Close but no cigar. The shooter emptied his gun, ejected the cartridge and took another from his pocket. In those couple of seconds it took to reload, Orla was immortal. She stepped out directly into his path, Jericho raised, and fired three times in quick succession.

The first two shots hit him square in the face.

The third missed because he wasn't there to be hit, he was already falling.

Six, she thought, both in terms of minutes and her total body count.

She tore across the corridor to the service door that led back to the stairs, and exploded through it in a flurry of controlled aggression. She kept the Jericho held out in front of her, ready to fire a fourth time. She swept the barrel up the stairs, ready to lay down a covering shot if needs be, and trying to see around the bannister. She kept her breathing absolutely regular. Easy. The mistake was to hold it. To think it would give you away. The world didn't work like that.

Satisfied there was no one waiting in ambush, she pounded down the stairs, taking them two and three at a time.

Five minutes thirty seconds, the clock in her head said. She needed to buy as much time as she possibly could, and she wasn't about to leave Jude's arse hanging out there waiting to be spanked.

At five minutes she was back on the floor with the CT lab.

She pushed the door open, but rather than step through it, waited. It was the smart move. Two bullets tore into door, a third splintered the frame.

The shooters were between her and Jude. That was less than ideal.

She fired blindly into the corridor, not caring where the bullets landed. She wanted the shooter to try to press his advantage. He did. She used the dark screen of Jude's tablet like a black mirror. The reflection was good enough to betray the shooter's position. Like a viper, Orla struck, letting off a double-tap of two shots before he even realised he was hit. The first took him in the gut, the second somewhere vital.

He went down, his rifle clattering to the floor as his hands betrayed him.

She retrieved the tablet and swung out into the corridor, sweeping through one eighty degrees, ready for others.

She didn't recognise the dead guy. She frisked him for ID, anything that would link him to Meyer or AI or anyone else. He was clean.

She still owed Jude four minutes at best, not that she actively wanted a fire fight in the corridors of the museum to earn them, but it was an effective way of killing time.

She crossed the floor to the lab.

Jude was gone.

"Fucker!" Orla grunted. She turned to go looking for him but Jude emerged from behind the door with his hands up.

"Don't kill me," he said, managing a grin despite the corpse in the corridor. He was a black humoured bastard sometimes, more like Noah Larkin than she cared to admit.

"Are you done?"

"If I say no?"

"We go anyway."

"I've found something."

"Save it. We're rolling."

She stashed the timber. Lethe handed her the thumb drive and in exchange he took the tablet back.

Together they left the room.

Orla covered him as he headed for the stairs, then backed him up, keeping her eyes fixed on the length of the corridor to ensure there were no nasty surprises.

She went through the fire doors into the stairwell first. The only way was up. She led the way, Jericho trained high. She moved quickly, shoulder scraping the wall as she turned the corner of the halfway landing.

"Incoming, two o'clock," Jude called, but Orla had already seen him.

The man was dead before he could raise his weapon, an angry red hole where his Adam's apple had been. He slumped and rolled, falling head first down the half a dozen steps to the landing. Jude sidestepped to avoid tripping on the corpse. The barked retort of her shot echoed up and down the stairwell for some time, filling it with noise.

And there went any hope of stealth.

They emerged on the ground floor, surrounded by glass-cased exhibits and statues and paintings that drew on the mythic nature of the city outside.

There was another guard sprawled out like a dead whore in the corridor. The first to die, presumably. Orla didn't bother checking him. The emergency services could do that when they responded to the alarm call. She told herself that a few seconds wouldn't make any difference, and almost believed the lie. She couldn't let herself worry about them. She was on mission. There was no room for sentimentality—or humanity.

There was no way they were walking out the front door.

Jude stayed close as she led the way, heading back to the service entrance they'd exploited for their entrance.

Two seconds later everything changed: three men came out of the security office.

They spotted Orla and Lethe immediately.

She took one out with a shot to the head before any of them could fire. Then she shoved Jude back towards the stairs. She caught a flicker of movement in the shadows and was forced to change direction, dragging Jude with her.

They had no choice but to take their chances with the museum proper.

She pushed open the crash doors.

The lighting here was dim, but the exit signs were bright. They served as guides along a red light road, past statues and display cases, pottery and other artefacts. Only the Artemision Bronze stood out, the impressively tall statue of either Zeus or Poseidon, nobody knew for sure. It stood at a crossroads in the exhibits. They took the right path, following the direction in which the statue appeared to be hurling something – a trident or a thunderbolt.

They *nearly* made it.

But nearly counted for fuck all in life and death.

The fire door was in sight.

Safety was that close.

Touching distance.

Two men stepped out from behind imposing sculptures, both ignoring Jude. They had their weapons trained on Orla.

She raised the Jericho ready to trade her life for theirs when more armed men closed in on them. Still more filled the exhibit hall behind them.

It was a fight she wasn't going to win.

Instead of pulling the trigger and raining down a few final deaths on the scales against her immortal soul, Orla Nyrén raised her hands into the air and allowed the Jericho to swing from her finger in the trigger guard.

"This is where I say we surrender?" Jude asked.

No one laughed.

Hands grabbed Orla roughly from behind. Someone took the Jericho.

Someone else threw a hessian bag over her head.

THIRTEEN

Tinnitus-like ringing in her ears echoed with terrible memories, masking what was real and what was not. It rose rapidly, spiralling to an eardrum-scratching pitch that had Orla shaking her head to be free of it. It was like trying to shake off the effects of a concussion grenade.

It masked the sound of muffled, heavy breathing.

Jude.

Breathing was a positive. It was much better than the alternative.

Her mouth was arid and sticky with the dull taste of blood. Nausea swum in her gut.

The hessian sack was rough against her skin. It reeked of dead fish, which only added to her nausea.

"Jude?" Orla said, expecting the sharp pain of someone cuffing her into silence.

Instead, the muffled noises increased, like he was wriggling around fighting his bonds. They'd almost certainly gagged him. Knowing Jude he'd brought that on himself.

"Do not talk. In fact, do not make a sound until you are told to make one." The voice was familiar, soft and caring like that of an old friend, though of course they were anything but friends.

"Enzo?"

"I warned you, my *Bellissima*," he told her as he lifted the bag from her head. There was genuine sorrow in his gaze. They were in a dark stone room with a single bare lightbulb hanging on a white plastic cord from the ceiling. Jude Lethe was tied to a chair, a blood-stained rag wrapped tightly around his mouth.

Orla tested her restraints.

"Why are you doing this?"

"It is not my doing, pretty lady," Enzo explained with a pained shrug, "and without *his* clumsy efforts," the giant Italian stared daggers at Jude, "I might have saved you. Now, I have no hope. I am not in control of the car, I am merely a passenger like you."

A noise sounded outside the cold room.

He stood over her, leaning in so close his lips brushed up against her ear as he whispered, "Give him what he wants and we get out alive," before he pulled away from her. The door opened and with it came the blistering heat of the desert air, followed by Adler Meyer. The fat man was sweating like over-ripened cheese left in the baking sun. He waddled into the room, threw his hat to the ground and reached into his coat for a condensation-laced bottle of water.

Noisily, he guzzled down half of it before emptying the rest and throwing the empty bottle away.

He wiped his mouth with the back of his hand.

His face was pink with anger, not just sunburn. He pointed at Enzo. "You, out," he ordered.

Without batting an eye, Enzo obeyed, leaving Orla and Jude alone with the seething Meyer.

As soon as the door closed, he rasped, "Do you have any idea how much *grief* you have caused me, *Yvonne*? Bloody fucking *woman!*" He raged and at Orla, fists shaking. "It was

105

stupid, stupid thing to do," he hissed, spittle flying from his lips, "Stealing from me!" He shook his head. "I should kill you."

She said nothing.

Meyer paced the ground between Orla and Jude, going back and forth between them. His feet were heavy on the hardened dirt.

He gripped a handful of his own sweaty hair, then punched at the air in frustration before continuing his tirade. "Did you really think that you could get away with it? Stupid, stupid woman. How could you not expect that we would track you to the very edges of the earth to retrieve it? Do you have any idea how much time you've *wasted*?"

He slammed a meaty hamhock of a fist into Orla's face. She rolled with the blow, spitting out a mouthful of blood. She didn't give him the satisfaction of flinching and begging. There was nothing to be gained from defying him. She simply waited for the next hammer blow. The wet sound of impact, of skin on skin, echoed off the cement walls.

Jude howled at the man, his scream lost in the gag.

"Shut the fuck up," Meyer levelled a stubby finger at Jude. "Or you will be silenced. Do you understand?"

Turning back to Orla, he pushed his face into hers, so close his nose bent as it came up against her cheek. "Why did you break into the museum?" He took both sides of her head in his fat hands. "Once chance, answer or I kill him."

Orla ignored the stream of blood seeping from her nose.

She wasn't fazed by the fat man's rage. She'd faced down beasts. He was a pig ripe for the slaughter. His heart would burst in his chest before he frightened her. Using his thumb he wiped the blood across her face.

"Speak, whore of Zeus."

Orla said nothing.

"Speak," he whispered like a lover, his hand making its way to her throat. He pressed his thumb against her trachea. "Are you so eager to die?"

Orla broke her silence. "Why should I tell you anything? You're going to kill us whatever I say. Or you'll try to."

He pulled away, his demeanor suddenly calm. He stared at her. "You're right," he said.

The cell was silent save for Jude's laboured breathing.

Meyer looked from her to Jude, then back again. He shrugged as if to say he'd given her every chance in the world to avoid this. He walked up behind Jude and covered his nose with those fat hands, clamping his nostrils shut.

Jude struggled against his restraints, fighting to suck air in through the gag.

He kicked at the legs of the chair and clawed at the armrests as he screamed through the precious little air he had.

Orla tried to stretch out the plastic cat stranglers that tied her to the chair, but the more she fought against them the tighter they became, biting deep enough to draw blood from her wrists. Even if she could have slewed off the top layer of skin and used the blood to lubricate her escape, it would have taken too long.

Jude wouldn't last without air. It was a pretty straightforward decision.

"Okay. I'll tell you," she said. No panic in her voice. No sense that she was actually surrendering, but those four words were enough for Meyer to release his grip on Jude's nose, allowing him to suck in the air his body so desperately craved.

"Speak," Meyer said again. He used that one word like a prayer.

"We were running the fragment of charred wood through the CT scanner, looking for some sort of next step, a clue, a secret message." Orla told him.

"And?"

"How the fuck would I know? People started shooting. I don't even know if he completed the scan before the goon squad turned up."

"You're lying."

"Big risk, that. Lying when you could so easily kill me. Besides, I don't really care. Believe whatever you want."

Meyer fell silent. He straightened his tie. It was a ludicrous affectation. It didn't make him appear any more gathered or in control. "Am I supposed to believe you are clueless to our intentions?"

Orla remained silent.

He reached for his bottle.

"We are going to dive to Heracleion."

"Why?"

"Don't play dumb. I know you have a copy of the journal. That means you know what we know. In fact, you know *more*, don't you? You snatched those wooden fragments from under our noses. At first, I admit, I couldn't believe it was you. But the footprints within the pit betrayed you. They were from a woman's shoe, and apart from your visit, we haven't had a single woman on site since we began excavations. It didn't take long to confirm the match for size. I decided to hunt you myself. I do so like the hunt. It's almost more fun than the kill."

"Stronger men than you have tried."

Meyer chuckled at this. "Actually, I'm lying. The only woman we've had on site is Yvonne Baudin. Both of them. The *real* Yvonne Baudin showed up the morning after you robbed us, which as you can imagine set a curious train of thought going, which, along with the tear sliced in the back of my tent and the dead man hiding under a tarp, led me to thinking. And I do so enjoy thinking. At first I assumed you were a detective, digging for clues as to who murdered the Petridis boy, but after a few enquiries, imagine my surprise when you turned out to be so very hard to identify."

"Imagine that," she said.

"It piqued my curiosity. In a life where two and two so rarely makes anything interesting, I at least had a corpse to examine for clues, and fingerprints all over several areas of my tent as well as the three dead men you'd already dispatched. So, I worked with what I had, a foreign woman fucking Petridis before he died. I knew it couldn't have been him who killed my boys. He couldn't even fight them off behind the bar. I'd dismissed you over and over." He chuckled again. "But no more. It wasn't easy, but I had you followed to the museum in Athens. And now, here you are, and now I need to decide what to do with you."

"Why not kill us?"

"It's always so blunt with people like you, isn't it?"

"Well you could let us go. I doubt you'd be up for that."

"You doubt correctly."

"What are you looking for in Heracleion?"

That surprised him. He inclined his head on the roll of fat around his neck. "You really don't know? So maybe your copy of the journal was incomplete. Your boy discovered there were three elements that when combined formed an ancient star chart. I have the disc and now I have the timbers. All I need that last fragment."

At the mention of the disc, Orla thought of Ares's necklace about her throat. She still felt the metal against her skin, or thought she did. She'd grown so used to it being there it was hard to tell. She didn't think that it was missing. So did that mean Meyer stole the original from the Heraklion Archeological Museum, or was he talking about a digital reproduction of it? Could he perhaps have found the real original Ares had talked about, which he had believed to be the same size as the gold replica Orla wore?

"When we reach Heracleion, my men will dive down to find a statue of Hercules," Meyer continued. "If my research is correct, as I believe it to be, there is a message hidden on it, the final piece of the triptych carried by the timbers and the Phaistos Disc. I haven't decided whether I will keep you alive long enough to see me fulfil my destiny, but you will be my whore before I end you."

"Of course I will. I'm hungry for your cock. Can't you tell? I'm just gagging for it. Newsflash, fat boy, I couldn't give a shit about your mystical star chart or your underwater statues. I want one thing."

"You aren't in a position to ask for anything, or bargain."

"And yet you're going to tell me."

"You seem sure of yourself."

"I am. Why did you kill him? Why did you kill Ares?"

The blare of a horn interrupted them.

Meyer looked up and then glanced at his watch. "Right on time. We need to leave now."

He threw open the cell door and issued a string of orders in guttural German. "Move them to the boat! We leave with the coming tide."

Four guards entered the room, one of them Enzo. He didn't bother masking his distaste when he saw what Meyer had done to Orla's face. He squatted down beside her, working on the ties. One of the other guards began to untie Jude's bonds.

"You–" Enzo kept his voice loud enough for the other guards to hear, "–will behave yourself, woman. No grief or I will throw you overboard." His eyes told a very different story to his words. He was playing to the cheap seats.

Orla nodded.

"Good, we understand each other." Enzo untied her feet and pulled her roughly to him. "Tie her hands," he ordered, still holding her while another guard carried out his bidding. Enzo leaned in and whispered in Orla's ear, the words so quiet she barely heard them.

"He was my friend."

It was as simple as that, and with those four words she was sure she had an ally in the big man.

Enzo retrieved the bag from the floor and pulled it down over Orla's head.

"Okay, let's go!" Enzo barked out the order, frog-marching Orla in front of him.

They walked into the hall and up a flight of stairs that led to the outside world.

The smell of sea filled the air; it was so strong it found its way through the rancid bag over her head. Sunlight filtered through the coarse fabric. Still daytime. She walked on wooden planks, meaning a jetty of some kind.

The waves buffeted the sides, but the walkway was stable.

A boat's motor started, a large boat by the sound of it.

Enzo lifted Orla off her feet.

She felt like a child in his giant arms.

He carried her onto the yacht and she felt him carry her up a flight of stairs to the upper decks. He set her down on a firm bench seat, and shouted more orders to his men. Another steroid enhanced grunt took a seat beside her, presumably to make sure she didn't try anything stupid like trying to make a swim for it.

Back on the shore Orla heard Meyer belching orders of his own.

The heavy footsteps of the guards thudded down the wooden walkway in response. She had no way of knowing if Lethe was with them, or if they'd left him behind to assure her cooperation.

"Where's my friend?" she asked.

Her guard shoved her shoulder.

"Zitto!" he growled.

"Jude?" Orla called, risking a beating.

"I suggest you be *very* quiet." Meyer's voice was much closer than she'd expected. "Your companion is quite safe. That is all you need to know."

Someone pulled the hessian sack from Orla's head. The sudden brightness had her squinting, eyes streaming from the sudden sting of the bright, bright light. She placed the sun; early evening. The yacht, an impressive luxury vessel, had already left the shore. She couldn't focus on the mass of tourists dotting the gold beach. They were little more than a hazy blur. Up on the top deck there was a bar, a swimming pool and a hot tub. It was decadent.

Orla tallied the guards, four on the deck, obviously more below. She could make a decent fight of it, but not yet. She needed to bide her time.

"Nice boat," Orla said.

"I enjoy the finer things in life," Meyer said, accepting a glass of cucumber flavoured water from his server. He eased back in his chair. "I am an important man. It is only right I possess the trappings of power."

"Is that so?"

"It is." He sipped at the ice water. "Are you important?"

"No."

His grip tightened on the glass. "I think you are. In fact, I think your employers would be willing to pay handsomely for your return."

"You really don't know the old man," a smirk spread across Orla's face at the thought of Sir Charles Wyndham dipping his hand into his wallet. He'd move heaven and earth to get her back, but he wouldn't actually *pay* good money for her. He really didn't like being strong-armed. It brought out the worst in him.

"That is too bad," he said, mocking her somberly. "Not that I actually would have delivered you. There's no fun in that."

She didn't answer.

She studied the fat man, taking in the micro-details of his face, then lingering on the brass buttons on his ivory-colored suit.

"What I still find myself wondering is why you got yourself involved? Why steal my timbers?" He squinted at her through the bright sun. "Of course you are a woman who causes me to wonder a lot of things, even things as basic as what your real name might be. Not that it matters. I am just a curious soul. You asked me why I killed Ares?"

"I guess we have something in common," Orla said, careful to keep her expression neutral.

"Do we?"

"I'm a curious soul."

"No," he imbued the simple syllable with so much derision and condescension, Orla's heartbeat quickened and she felt her rage build. "That's not it at all, is it? What? Did you actually care for him? Is that it? Oh how deliciously pathetic. You cared."

"You think you've figured me out?"

"The mysterious woman in red is not so mysterious after all." He took another sip of his drink, relishing the fact that everyone around him was baking in the sun while he dripped sweat in the shade. "You are just like every other miserable bitch on this God-forsaken planet, predictable and disappointing."

"Why did you kill him?"

"Tsk, tsk," he tutted. "*I* didn't kill him at all. Look at me. I could hardly do away with a physical specimen like Ares Petridis. No, no, your boy was outgrowing his boots. He needed humbling. Especially as he was becoming precious with his secrets. I do so hate secrets. I think it was his mother's doing, he had such an Oedipal thing going on with mummy."

"So murder's your stock in trade? Someone becomes a liability, kill them?"

"Not all. I am a fair ruler of my minions, just as I will be a fair ruler of Greece."

"Come again?"

"And spoil the surprise? Consider this, since the monarchy was abolished in the seventies, Greece's fortunes have fallen somewhat. I think perhaps it is time to return to the old ways."

"You can't be serious."

"Would you like to be my queen?"

Meyer found this hilariously funny. Orla shook her head. She could have thrown herself at him, broken the fat man's neck before his people could react, but that wouldn't solve anything. It went beyond the fat man and his megalomania. He was only one of the players. So for now she'd let him live.

The roar of a motor boat pulling up alongside Meyer's yacht was accompanied by the staccato rattle of gunfire.

Orla took cover.

Meyer yelled useless orders, demanding the intruders be killed, over and over yelling "Kill them!"

She made three men on the other boat. They fired indiscriminately at Meyer's yacht, not caring who or what they hit as glass shattered and upholstery was ripped to shreds all across the upper deck. The shots were ineffectual in terms of reducing the numbers. None of them hit the mark. Meyer's men took cover. One of the men, who scrambled away from the hail of gunfire in Orla's direction as bullets punched holes in the lifeboat behind him.

Orla hooked a hand around his ankle, making sure he pitched forward face first, sprawling across the deck. She was on his back in a heartbeat, snatching his gun from its holster and smashing the butt into his man's temple several times until he stopped moving.

Taking up position, she crouched behind the low wall around the foredeck.

Orla laid down controlled bursts of fire to take out another of Meyer's men.

They didn't expect the enemy within their ranks. They were all focussed on the attack from the sea, as amateurish as it was.

The second boat was smaller, built for pursuit. There were no coastguard or police markings. That meant someone had hired this crew to come after Meyer.

Best guess? The black widow, Mother Petridis. If Meyer was following Orla, why not Maria, too? It made a grim kind of sense that everyone would be watching her whilst she led them towards the answers. Perhaps this was a rescue attempt.

Unfortunately for them, whoever hired the other boat, they'd vastly underestimated the number of men at Meyer's command. It wasn't going to end well for them. Three of

Meyer's goons stood on the edge of the yacht's upper deck, spraying the smaller boat with gunfire in return. Nobody from the other boat returned fire; not a good sign.

She risked checking. No one appeared to be steering the craft. It just bumped up against the side of their hull over and over, bushed into the yacht by the tide.

After a time, they left the enemy boat trailing in their wake.

Orla stayed low, watching Meyer's remaining men check on the dead.

In the noise and fury of the attack, they hadn't realised that several of the kill shots had come from her. She wasn't about to plug the gap in their knowledge.

Meyer screamed more orders.

She saw that Enzo was up on deck.

He did the fat man's bidding without question.

"Find the bitch!" Meyer howled.

She enjoyed his discomfort. She contemplated jumping overboard, but that just made a target of her and meant leaving Jude behind. That wasn't happening. The two lifeboats on the upper deck were riddled with bullet holes. She couldn't see the third and fourth boats on the lower deck from where she was—it was a risk to assume they were sea worthy. And even if they were, that meant finding Jude, assuming he was below decks somewhere, then pulling off the ridiculous exfiltration that concluded with liberating a lifeboat and a high speed nautical chase.

It was the kind of thing Noah would do.

She wasn't Noah.

But she couldn't just sit on her arse. She had to do *something*. If nothing else, he'd expect it of her, and she didn't want to disappoint.

She watched Meyer's goons scour the deck for her.

Enzo and another man disappeared below decks, no doubt checking to be sure she hadn't decided to take advantage of the chaos and tried to liberate Jude.

She watched the search team sweep the deck. She could have taken them all down if she'd got the bullets. She had no idea how many shots were left in her stolen gun. Judging from the weight she guessed she had six or seven shots remaining. She could do a lot of damage with those. But she hesitated. It wasn't just about giving her position away. There was more to it than that. Timing was everything. It was a zero sum game. One stray bullet ended it all. One lucky shot.

She climbed nimbly over the railing of the top deck, tucking the stolen weapon into the back of her jeans. Moving swiftly, Orla lowered herself, adjusting her position so she hung at full stretch, then let go, dropping to the lower deck.

She landed softly.

Drawing the weapon again, she stalked silently towards the door to the interior.

She wasn't sure where Jude was held, if he was even on board, but it wasn't *that* big a boat. She'd find him if he was there to be found.

Silently, she opened the door and ducked inside. A narrow corridor ran the length of the boat, with several closed doors leading into cabins. The easy way to tell if they were occupied was to open the doors. Sometimes keeping things simple was the best way to go. Orla moved down the corridor, systematically moving from cabin to cabin. The first was a communal bathroom, the next a galley kitchen. She reached the last door before the ladder to the upper deck.

She pushed the door open.

On the bed sat a bald headed man with a black goatee, his wrists were handcuffed around metal pillar. Orla recognised him from the dig; he was one of the men who had argued with Meyer before the fat man killed his companion. She searched for his name.

"Siegfried?"

His eyes widened.

"Who are you?"

"My name is Orla. I'm looking for my friend?"

Siegfried looked troubled. Not like a man being saved. Far from it, he looked like a man who had just been condemned.

He didn't offer any sort of answer, he merely pointed up towards the ceiling.

The huge window was open to the sky, and the fat man leered down at her through the opening. "Well, well, well, now I know your name, at least. Why don't you come back up to deck, Orla? Your friend wants to say goodbye before he tries to outswim the sharks. I will, of course, cut him first, work them up into a frenzy with his blood. Otherwise there's no sport."

"I'll be back, don't go anywhere," she told the prisoner, and backed out into the corridor and straight into the glowering Enzo. The big man took the gun from her with a sigh.

"Sorry *Bellissima*. You are giving me a headache. He will demand I hurt you now."

"You don't have to," she said.

"I do."

FOURTEEN

Jude wasn't dead yet.

Yet.

It was a powerful word. It meant there was a world of possible outcomes still on the table.

He sat in the corner, worrying at loose threads on a bedsheet, looking thoroughly miserable. She nodded to him, trying to communicate a wealth of information silently.

Siegfried was equally disconsolate.

Whatever uneasy truce he'd had with Meyer was history.

"Orla Nyrén," she said, not caring if anyone knew her name. There was no power in it. This wasn't some mystical rite. It made no difference if Meyer knew who killed him or not. "Why are you being held captive? From the argument I overheard I thought you were partners? You don't have to answer, but knowing the truth might help me."

"We are. Or were. If you don't kowtow to the man you're on his list. You must immediately agree with Adler or he considers you a liability. It wasn't supposed to be like this. This mess. This whole thing. I wish I'd never listened when he came to me with his ridiculous plan. Hunting relics through the stars... have you ever heard the like?" The man sighed dejectedly.

"What is he hunting?"

"He believes that when the triptych is combined it will reveal the location of one of most famous relics of Greek antiquity. A treasure once possessed by Jason himself, the fleece of the magical ram that once belonged to Zeus himself."

"The Golden Fleece?"

Jude said, "I had my suspicions, but they were pretty much confirmed when I saw the markings revealed by the CT scan; a map of the stars in the constellation Argo Navis."

"I don't know that constellation."

"Because it isn't called that any more. Argo Nevis was the constellation created when the Argo was raised into the skies. Once it became obvious we were on a treasure hunt linked to that constellation, with the Argo itself leading the way, what else could it be?"

"Okay, a golden fleece. His talk was all about power not money. What kind of power can a fleece convey?" When no one answered her, she tried a different line of questioning. "Ask yourself this, why did Meyer kill Ares? Not why does he say he did it, because it's not about refusing to share information. That can't be the entire reason, so why?"

Siegfried's face betrayed his torment. He buried his face in his hands. "That poor boy," he mumbled.

Orla watched him struggle with his grief.

He rocked back and forth gently, like a child in desperate need of comforting.

She didn't move. He knew something. Silence was the interrogator's best weapon with the weak; let them find the words to fill it.

"He was my protégé," Siegfried said at last, "my star pupil. Now, because of me, he is dead."

Still, she said nothing, waiting for his confession to take shape.

"I brought him on to this project. I filled his head with the romance of it. I was his archeology professor at the university. He had a real passion for the subject. He was a bright, shining star. He introduced me to his parents who took great interest in my work and wanted to support their son. They offered us the use of their ships to help transport our finds. Ares was pursuing his passion, and that was my fault. He should have stayed working for his father. How could I know it would end like this? That this farce would get him killed?"

And still Orla said nothing.

Confession is good for the soul.

Siegfried tried to smile, his red eyes weary and sad. "I was in love with him, you know?"

His admission took Orla by surprise, but she didn't interrupt. "We all were, I suppose; everyone who encountered him fell in love with him in some way. The boy was the embodiment of everything it meant to be Greek, I swear. He was all of our gods brought back in one charismatic, charming, beautiful body. God I miss him."

"Sounds like a catch," Jude said.

Siegfried looked at him, not understanding the double edged barb to the seemingly flippant comment. "Smart, handsome, full of life and eager to experience it. Yes. He would have been. Not that he knew we loved him. He never would have understood how we could be drawn to him, so helpless and desperate to be in his shade." Siegfried rubbed his hands together. "I suppose, in the face of death, one can say what they like."

"So you were his mentor?" Orla said, finally breaking her silence.

"Yes. The dig was mine initially. I invited him onto the team and eventually put him in charge. When he confided in me that he believed he had deciphered the remaining symbols on the Phaistos Disc, I admit I panicked and flew back to Corinth. I feared, deep in my soul, that Adler would not allow two archeologists to advance to the next stage of the initiative. I just wasn't able to conceive the lengths to which he would go... and some small part of me refused to believe. By the time I arrived, it was too late. He left the dig – cut himself off from the rest of us, and then he drowned. When Hans found out, he confronted us and Adler shot him. He murdered his friend of thirty years in cold blood. He didn't so much as bat an eyelid. He just pulled the trigger. I know I'm next. I am not a fool. Once Adler knows where to find the Fleece my usefulness will be over."

"How long have you known him?"

"We studied together at university. So the answer to your question is a long time. We were inseparable. Both of us dreamed of discovering the greatest lost treasures of our society. It fuelled our blood. It was our passion. And then one summer, he sojourned in Italy with his parents. When he returned, he was different. Obsessed with control and money. He altered our plans. He wanted to sell the relics we found to the highest bidder instead of putting them in museums for all of our people to enjoy." His hands began to shake. "I was weak. This change in him frightened me. He introduced me to Hans who worked for Argo International, who provided the funds for our excavations... Now he's dead and Adler is out of control."

"He dreams of being king," Orla told him.

"King? Of Greece? That's ludicrous. There is no monarchy."

"He wants it reinstated."

"Stay with me here," Jude interrupted, "But I think I'm joining the dots—or stars—we know there's no such thing as magic, but the fleece is obviously of significant cultural value. It's the kind of symbol that can rally a people, like the Seal of Solomon. You said Maria claimed her lineage was from Theseus, right? And that there's two sides to every story?"

"Three."

"Okay, three, but forget Hercules for now, what if Meyer believes he is descended from Jason? Or intends to make that claim? Two great families colliding over the future of their nation, joined throughout antiquity in the greatest tales? One of them wants to be king, I'd be on board. I love a good story. I'm not the only one. A legend like that, coming to life? It's got power."

"Meyer's German!" Orla said.

Siegfried answered. "Adler's grandfather was Greek. He was captured during the War and taken to Germany. After the war he settled there. His mother had a Greek name, I forget it now, but she married a German man and Adler was born in Germany."

"We're getting way ahead of ourselves here. We can't know any of this stuff. Even speculating about it is just racing off down blind alleyways. And right now the why isn't important. It's the how that matters."

"Soon though we will know more and it will be the death of us. He intends to have his men dive down to the statue and uncover the inscription. Once I construct the star chart and reveal the location of the Fleece, he'll probably kill me. Now, I have told you all I know. All I fear. I have one question for you, if you would do me the courtesy? Who are you? Police? Special Forces? Who do you work for? Why are you here?"

"I was on holiday, and that's more than one question," Orla replied.

Siegfried leaned toward her, his gray eyes questioning. "You can get us out of here, can't you?"

"I'm not David Blaine," she said. "We're in the middle of the ocean. There's nowhere to go."

They were interrupted by the arrival of Adler Meyer. Enzo and two other armed men squeezed in behind him.

Meyer addressed Siegfried.

"Well? Did she spill her guts to you, my friend?"

Orla and Jude stared daggers at Siegfried, who appeared to shrink before their eyes.

Meyer pushed for information. "I'm sure they gave you something useful?"

Orla watched the old man whose knees shook so badly he could barely stand. "I have no interest in your delusions of grandeur."

Meyer hesitated, his piggy eyes scanning his friend up and down, his gaze coming to rest on Siegfried's shaking knees.

"What have you done?" he demanded "What have you told them?"

"Nothing!" Siegfried's tone was anything but persuasive.

"You always were a bad liar. You weak, weak fool. You disappoint me, old friend. How pathetic you have become." Shaking his head, he turned to Orla.

"And you, my dear, I know you shot some more of my men while we were under attack. I'd break your neck right now except you killed one of my most experienced divers. I hope you are proficient with SCUBA gear because you're going down with what's left of my team."

"Am I?"

"Yes you fucking well are. And your friend can go down with you to keep you honest."

"Oh, now, wait," Jude protested, but Meyer had already stormed from the room. Enzo and the other two followed, locking the door behind them.

Siegfried stared through the floor. "I didn't know he would ask me that," he said. "I am a dead man. I will take your secrets to my watery grave, I swear."

The silence that followed his denial was far from comfortable.

Jude cleared his throat. "So, aside from swimming with the fishes, what's the plan?" he asked.

Orla scanned the room for any possible means of escape. "I don't have a plan."

"You *always* have a plan," Jude said.

"I think we'll be able to get away when we dive," Orla replied. "We won't be alone, but it's going to be our best shot." It was unfair on Jude, but she couldn't help but wish she was trapped in here with any of the others on the team, Konstantin, Ronan or Noah. She would never say that to him. She didn't need to. He knew. How could he not?

"You do not need to save me. There is nothing to save. I am dying," Siegfried confessed. "I have been for a long time. Adler does not know. There is a tumour the size of a grapefruit in my lungs. I am sixty-six years old and I will not see sixty-seven. Use me. I would like to do some good before I go." He gazed at Orla imploringly. "Make me your weapon."

She sighed. "Unless I can load you with bullets and mow down Meyer's minions, I'm not sure I can use you."

FIFTEEN

"You're looking for a giant statue, obviously there are several down there. There should be patterns on it similar in nature to those on the timber from the Argo and on the Phaistos Disc."

The buttons of Meyer's shirt strained against his expansive gut, showing a wire of black hairs and the pale skin in the light of the full moon. He gripped the side rail as the boat lurched up and down in the choppy waters.

Orla and Jude wore wetsuits.

Meyer's men prepped their SCUBA gear, running through the various safety checks.

Siegfried stood to one side, nervously fiddling with his fingers because his hands had nothing to do.

"Siegfried has done extensive inventory checks with the various museums and authorities involved in the find," Meyer continued, "and not a single statue of Hercules has been brought to the surface yet, which leads us to assume it is still down there, though we have no photographs to confirm that supposition. According to the GPS readout we're positioned directly above the temple of Herakles, which is the most logical place to begin looking."

"You'd think," Lethe said.

"Once you find the statue, you are to photograph the markings and return to the surface."

"You make it sound so straight forward." Jude's sarcasm rippled up the ladder to Meyer. "And then let me guess, you kill us? I feel like you should be sitting there stroking a cat and twirling your moustache. Maybe you want to bark out a *mwahaha* kind of laugh while you're at it?"

"Your fate is already sealed, don't whine like a bitch." Meyer paused to belch loudly, swallowing back whatever had crawled back up his throat.

"Excuse you," Jude said, adjusting the Velcro strap across his chest. He'd checked and rechecked it half a dozen times already.

"I notice you're not coming," Orla said.

Lethe stage-whispered, "It's physics. He's a fat fuck. That means he's buoyant. He'd never get down there."

Meyer was not amused.

"Time to go," he said, as though dispensing a punishment for Jude's barbed tongue. He signalled the five men in diving gear. "You have enough air for one hour."

The divers set their wristwatches accordingly.

Orla and Jude didn't have watches.

Neither did they have daggers strapped to their calves.

"This is going to be fun," Jude said. He didn't get to say anything more because one of the divers shoved him over the side of the boat without warning. He disappeared beneath the black surface of the water.

Orla rolled off the side of the boat. As soon as she hit the water she felt the familiar claustrophobia, that muscle memory of water flooding into her nose and mouth, that she couldn't breathe, and would die in silent desperation.

Meyer's men followed one after the other.

127

She tasted the water, realising that Aboukir Bay was filthy and full of garbage. Rubbish floated all around her. A film of something unpleasant clung to the surface. It reeked. She shuddered, grateful for the wetsuit.

It was only thirty feet down to the sea bed.

She swam over to Jude, and helped him check his regulator and ensure his mask was fitted correctly before sorting out her own equipment.

Jude took the regulator out of his mouth. "I don't think I can do this."

Orla placed her hands on his shoulders and looked him in the eye. "I know about Peru. I know what you did. I know all about Lima, all of it. Frost told me. You can do this. This is just a swim. See the sights and come back up again. Over before you know it. Don't worry about the rest. I've got you. Okay?"

He nodded. "Okay."

The men were ready.

One of them gave the signal for the others to dive.

She ruffled Jude's hair, then put back her regulator.

"Was that strictly necessary?" he said, twisting his lips. She nodded. He put in his own, and together they dived down under the surface of the Mediterranean Sea.

During the day, the sea could be a beautiful turquoise masterpiece. By night, it was something different altogether, something menacing and ominous.

The dive leader switched on the flashlight attached to his mask and released the air in his BCD.

Orla, Jude and the other four mirrored him and they began their descent.

Dropping through the inky water, she was shocked at how murky even these shallow depths were. The beams from their headgear cut trails through the fogged water, but could only penetrate so far into the murk before fading no more than a couple of metres in front of their faces.

Beyond that was blackness.

It was only going to get worse the deeper they went.

Orla equalised as the pressure mounted, popping her ears and controlling her breathing. She signalled Jude, giving him the okay sign. He raised his own hand, thumb and forefinger pressed together in a ring. All good. She wished she was telling the truth. Tendrils of panic coiled around her mind, trying to force their way in, squeezing at her. She saw the Beast in the black, she saw the rancid mattress, the blood slick cell walls, and remembered the pig's trough in which they forced her head under the water, holding her down to the point of drowning, and bringing her back, over and over. The dark water held all of her demons.

She would not give into it. Not then. Not now. Not ever.

She drew Meyer's grotesque features in her mind.

There would come a point where all of these old debts he had accrued would be paid off. And that would be the death of him.

They reached the sea bed.

The distant moonlight diffused the scene, transforming the water into a creepy graveyard fog. Their flashlights helped dispel some of the gloom, but nowhere near enough.

Sediment kicked up as the divers landed on the sea bed.

Orla negotiated a series of ropes and flags the archaeologists had used to section off the dig site. She looked towards Jude. He seemed to be keeping it together. She pointed downwards. He followed her directions, the flashlight illuminating the ropes at his feet.

He gave her the thumbs up. It was tough to see the motion in the gloom despite the fact that if they'd both reached out they could have touched fingertips, so dark and dense was the water.

She swam closer, reaching out for his hand.

He squeezed her fingers through the gloves and she returned the gesture.

The dive leader joined them. He had a wickedly sharp blade in his right hand that he used to point off into the murk. The meaning was obvious; the clock was ticking.

Adjusting her buoyancy, she levelled out and used her flippers to propel herself forward.

Jude, still holding her hand, followed her lead.

The dive leader brought up the rear.

The other four divers paired up and headed out in different directions.

The lost city spanned over eleven kilometres in total. They could be searching for a lifetime if Meyer's calculations were off.

They swam on.

Orla surveyed the sea bed, sweeping the flashlight's beam with gentle turns of the head. It was like coral beneath them, but unnaturally regular. It took her a moment to realise she was looking at a collapsed section of wall. The blocks of stone covered in crustaceans and seaweed still held their shape even horizontal across the ground. Could it be a perimeter wall from the Temple of Herakles?

A shape loomed out of the dark and Orla pulled up sharply.

She stared at an awe inspiring sight.

Less than two metres away, the enormous object was much too large to be a person, yet it was man-shaped.

Moving closer, her light fell on a face with a tube-like beard and headdress. The ancient pharaoh gazed at her through the depths.

It was incredible.

She glanced sideways. Jude's face caught in her light, was full of reverence and awe.

The craftsmanship was incredible. The carving was a thing of beauty, a little worn in places but very much preserved by the salt water.

But as impressive as he was, the subject wasn't Hercules.

They had to move on.

More giant statues loomed in the murky waters, along with countless broken amphorae and vases.

Any portable objects still intact had long since been taken to the surface.

As she swam, she divided her attention between watching over Jude and following the guide ropes, noting section numbers on the flags to ensure they didn't cover the same ground twice. It was so dark they had no choice but to search metre by metre, following a painstaking grid. And even then, the chances of finding anything were predicated very much on Meyer's calculations and luck.

And even if they found a statue of the legendary warrior there was no guarantee it was the statue they were looking for. It felt like a hopeless task. Orla ran the beam of her flashlight along the sandy floor, picking out giant, broken pots and blocks of stone. She couldn't be sure how long they'd been down there, or how far from the boat they'd travelled. It was all guess work. She hated guess work. That wasn't who she was. It was like scrabbling in the mud with her bare hands for the timbers all over again.

They searched on.

Treasures that would make the old man weep littered the sea bed.

A few patches of the sand were bereft of artefacts, large holes backfilled with a slide of silt where statues once stood.

On and on they swam.

It was impossible; a needle in a watery grave of a haystack.

She checked the valve on the air tank, over two-thirds gone, meaning they'd been down here forty minutes or so. They had maybe twenty minutes at best before they had to surface.

She was due some luck.

The sea bed became gradually more and more regular, smooth, with stones seemingly arranged in neat lines. They followed the lines, realising soon that the stones were in fact stacked, rising upwards like a staircase. A minute or so later she found herself swimming in through the arch of a ruined structure. There was no roof, and the walls had partially collapsed, but it was unmistakably a grand building, or had been before it was submersed.

Could it be the Temple of Herakles?

The dive leader checked a map. He wasn't paying attention to her.

The thought of pulling his air crossed her mind; he'd be easy to drown, but even if she killed him there were the others, and the problem of what to do when they got back to the surface And then there was Jude. If she made a move down here, they wouldn't try to stop her, they'd go for her weak spot: him. That effectively meant she had to just play along, biding her time, and biding it some more. Maybe Meyer was smarter than he looked, sending an inexperienced diver like Jude Lethe down here with them.

The floor of the temple was covered in silt and fine sand. At times she lost sight of the external walls and had no way of knowing if she'd drifted outside of the building. But then she would see something, a broken statue, a carved stone, and she knew she was likely still within its confines.

She swam on.

There was something strange protruding from the floor beneath her; a spike, not unlike the crown of the statue of liberty, sprouted from beneath the sand. Most of it, whatever it was, was beneath a large stone. The rounded points were coated with green slime and the beginnings of self-planted seaweed.

She dug around the tips, pushing the sand back with her gloved hand.

What she'd thought was a crown turned out to be the mane of a lion.

She struggled to move the stone so she could better get to the statue beneath, but there was no way she could lift it on her own. Almost as soon as the thought crossed her mind, she was suddenly surrounded by other divers who'd converged on her location.

Together, they managed to lift the stone. It was like the capstone on a well, moving it exposed a lot more of the statue, letting it be seen for the first time in centuries. They dug around it, all hands pawing away at the body and head, churning up so much silt and sand as to render visibility extremely limited. It took almost half a minute for the sediment to settle and for Orla to see that they'd uncovered the head of a lion perched upon the head of a powerful giant slayer of a man. She knew the legends; Hercules was the embodiment of strength, often depicted battling a mighty lion or wearing its pelt as a symbol of its defeat.

Everyone helped her now, even Jude, digging deeper to expose even more of the statue.

A minute later they'd clumsily excavated all the way down to expose the middle of the statue's immense torso. The sculpt was beautiful. The man in the lion coat that hugged his shoulders was divine in more ways than one. This was a statue fit for a god, the subject more than any mere mortal.

The dive leader tapped his watch and pointed upwards.

Orla shook her head.

Desperate to find some sign of the mysterious markings, she ran hands up and down the exposed shoulder, across the lion's coat, using her fingertips to dig into the corroded crust over the stone, feeling out any irregularities that might be engravings.

Working her hands towards Hercules's head, she closed her eyes and pulled off her glove, letting her fingers guide her. She felt her way around the carved muscles, not sure what she was looking for until she found it; a square with two diagonal slices carved deep into it. Astonishingly, after all these years beneath the water, the square moved an inch inwards when she applied pressure.

The back of the statue ground stone against stone, a flurry of bubbles rising as ancient air trapped within found an escape. Under the lights of the assembled divers, they watched as a panel in Hercules's spine cranked opened.

Orla brushed a layer of seaweed away, and repositioned herself over the statue's back to peer into the cavity within.

The flashlight illuminated the interior.

And there it was, plain and perfect as the day they had been carved: a series of odd patterns, much like those on the Disc and the timbers.

The dive leader shoved her roughly out of the way.

The water stopped her going far, but the indignity of it made her wish she had a knife, too. The dive leader took out an underwater camera and motioned for two of his fellows to light up the interior of the statue.

He took a number of photographs from every angle.

And that was it, time to leave.

Orla made ready to adjust her buoyancy to rise back to the surface, but she noticed Jude, almost invisible in the darkness, signalling furiously to her.

The dive leader and the others were already ascending.

Orla swam across to the leader, grabbing his arm and gesticulating frantically to draw his attention to Jude. To her horror he shoved her away and up they went. They'd got what they wanted, nothing else mattered.

Orla swam over to Jude. His flipper was caught under the rock they'd shifted to get at the statue. His was pinned, and his air was running out. Fear had him breathing faster, a cloud of bubbles erupting from his regulator.

Orla moved in close so that he could see her face by his torchlight.

Her mask was inches from his. She reached out her hands to hold his arms, willing him to be calm.

He stared at her in panic. She could see his wide eyes. She tapped her regulator, trying to get him to understand that he needed to get his breathing under control, then pointed two fingers in a V-shape to Jude's eyes, then turned them to point to her own. *You watch me.*

He nodded, his eyes fixed on hers. Still panicking.

She made a deliberate show of breathing, keeping it steady and showing him a rhythm to copy.

He struggled to emulate her.

The bubbles reduced, the trail thinning out. A moment or two later he seemed much more in control. That was good. It was a start. Jude wasn't going to die down here, she wouldn't let him.

She held up a finger. *One moment.* Then she pointed downward.

He nodded, clearly concentrating on his breathing.

She ducked down to his feet.

The rock had taken seven of them to lift. She was on her own.

There was no way she was moving it.

Instead she reached around Lethe's ankle and loosened the strap on his flipper. It wasn't easy, fumbling blindly, but she managed to release it and pull his bare foot free.

He kicked out for the surface, travelling far too quickly.

Orla shot after him, grabbing his leg as he swam with all his might towards the air.

There was nothing wrong with his equipment, Orla knew. It was pure reflex. Panic still hot in his veins.

She had to stop him before he reached the surface or the nitrogen release was going to do serious damage to his body. Too far, too fast. He wasn't giving himself time to decompress and process the nitrogen in his blood. Orla was a stronger swimmer and had the advantage of two flippers. She drew level with him and forced him to focus on her face again, weighing down on his shoulders. She forced him to stop fighting her, to look at her even as more bubbles streamed out of his mask. Thirty seconds. One minute. She counted out the heartbeats before she took his hand and they ascended together.

Jude kept his eyes locked on hers.

Orla broke contact for a moment, getting her bearings. They were level with the five enemies, who were waiting to equalise before breaking the surface. They'd come up that fast. She wasn't happy. If she surfaced with Jude, Meyer would have no further use for either of them. He was likely waiting up there with a rifle in his fat hands, ready to shoot them as soon as they came near the boat. If she was going to do something, now was the time. She'd faced worse odds.

Admittedly not while underwater, but she liked a challenge, and she knew how to gain an advantage over her opponents.

She pointed at the other divers and made a stabbing motion, so Jude would see her intentions. He nodded, his breathing still ragged but under control. She indicated he should stay put and that she would return. Then she gave him the thumbs up and kicked away from him.

She clicked off her light so they wouldn't see her coming and glided up behind the nearest of the men like a circling shark.

In the darkness, he and his friends couldn't see her until it was too late.

Orla popped open the strap holding the man's knife in its leg-holster, then she whipped out the blade, filling the water with arterial spray as the man bled out. His blood was the colour of ink, the contrast more obvious at this depth than it might have been nearer the sea bed.

Using the dying man's body as a shield, she positioned herself so the nearest diver couldn't see her. He was heading for Jude's light, assuming it was her.

She was more than prepared to let Jude serve as a decoy for as long as it took to kill the second man.

He ghosted past her position, noticing the danger too late.

Orla pushed away from her human shield, arrowing herself through the dark water at the unsuspecting diver. Her corpse springboard sank out of sight into the gloom as she reached his still-living friend.

Her stolen blade slashed through his regulator line before he could react, taking him out of the fight with an explosion of bubbles. No one could hear his distress through the dampening effect of the water. She couldn't let him surface, so as his foot passed her head she stabbed it clean through with her blade. He thrashed about in panic, trying to kick out at her. Orla used her free hand to grab a handful of his wetsuit at the knee, then she pulled herself up the length of his body. Her blade stabbed into his thigh, then withdrew as she hoisted herself up, pulling him down, climbing him like a mountaineer scaling the rock face with an axe to make handholds. The next stab of her knife punctured his chest and he went limp. She adjusted his BCD and he sunk like a stone statue.

Two down.

She'd lost count of how many dead she'd accumulated on her vacation, but it had to be close to a dozen, or would be by the time she was finished.

The third diver had nearly reached Jude. She powered after him, driven by her determination not to let any harm come to her friend.

He was only inches from Jude as she took him from behind.

He struggled to push her away until she rammed the blade into his neck and sliced outwards, creating a fan-like arc that rippled out through the water, holding its shape like a spray of modern art on a living—dying—canvas. More of the man's vital fluids flooded outwards creating more artwork as the diver's heart pumped out blood under pressure.

Orla ducked beneath the cloud before it could blind her.

Three down.

The last two, including the dive leader, were wise to Orla's threat.

They came at her.

She backed away, her blade held ready. It rippled through the water between them as her arm seemed to move in slow motion.

Two together wasn't great.

She retreated again, pushing back against the current.

One went over her head, kicking up and gliding by, out of range of her knife.

She didn't even try to cut him.

The other dived went lower, moving beneath her.

This wasn't going to end well.

She had to make a choice. High was better. She kicked upwards, aiming at intercepting the man above her. The dive leader was experienced and agile, unlike his bulky colleagues, and twisted away from her, using the water to his advantage. Her slash was too slow, the movement laboured. He kicked out in return, his flippered foot in her face.

She tried to bring the knife around to stab his calf, but it was next to impossible against the resistance of the water. He kicked back, knocking the regulator from her mouth.

A third kick to her wrist sent the knife spinning out of reach before she could grab it again.

He twisted in the water like an eel, darting around to come for her head first. His knife glittered in the crossbeam from his flashlight.

Orla struggled to hold him, arms locked together in a deadly dance as the dive turned into a violent ballet.

Neither could gain an advantage.

The difference was that he still had his regulator and she could only hold her breath so long. She needed to get the regulator back into her mouth soon, otherwise she was going to be in trouble.

The second swimmer, the one who had gone beneath her, kicked away, swimming powerfully across the distance to where Jude's light blazed erratically. He was trying to escape, but with only one flipper he was nowhere near as fast as his pursuer.

She had her own problems.

She felt the bite of the knife as it carved a slice out of her arm.

Blood leaked into the water like an oil spill.

She focussed on the pain.

It calmed her natural urge to take a breath.

Orla's strength was waning but her resolve held firm.

They grappled on, kicking and twisting. The bubbles from his regulator raced towards the surface.

The knife cut more flesh from her arm, but she didn't panic. It was only pain. She could cope with pain. She'd lived with a world of it.

She curled her legs in tight to her chest, and then kicked out with all her might.

The blow connected under his chin. His head snapped back, the regulator falling from his mouth. The shock of the impact had him instinctively sucking down a huge mouthful of water as he struggled to catch a breath that wasn't there, and that only exacerbated the struggle.

He was clearly in distress.

She climbed up his body, twisting herself around, using the buoyancy to do impossible things, her legs wrapped around his shoulders as she was behind his head. She grabbed the cobra-like regulator as it lashed about wildly, and pulled it tight under his neck, choking him as she ducked in close to his ear to suck on the air valve, intending to breathe life-giving air even as she choked the life out of him. She breathed out, clearing her mouth of water, then took a deep breath in, then out, drawing down half a dozen long lungfuls of sweet air as she pinned him.

He slashed at her with his knife and punched with his free hand, each blow weaker than the last. The angle made it next to impossible for him to hurt her beyond puncturing her suit.

Orla took out the regulator, tightening the cord around the man's neck, and pulled with all her might until she finished it.

It took fifteen seconds.

She could have held her breath for considerably longer.

She clung onto the dead man long enough to reclaim his underwater camera from where it was clipped to his suit.

She grabbed his knife then released him, watching for a second or two as he drifted listlessly towards the ruins of Heracleion.

She retrieved her own regulator, put it back in her mouth.

It was so dark it was hard to see Jude.

She kicked out in the direction she saw him go, but there was no sign of his light.

Now she was worried.

She swam around as long as the air would allow, searching desperately for him.

There was no light, not his, not the diver who'd gone for him. The presence of one would have meant he was down on the sea bed, the absence of both suggested he was up on the surface. She chose to be optimistic.

Her tank was down to its last dregs of air.

Adjusting her BCD, Orla swam upwards.

She broke the surface, removing her regulator to taste real air for the first time in an hour. It had never tasted so good. Taking deep breaths, she turned her head wildly left and right scanning the water for any sign of her companion.

The boat was about fifty metres away and drifting.

In the moonlight she could see several figures on deck. None of them could see her. She made Enzo first, then Meyer and lastly, thankfully, Jude.

She swam cautiously closer, each stroke near silent in the night.

Nobody tried to shoot her.

As she neared the boat she could see the knife reflecting the light of the moon, held against Jude's throat.

"I sincerely hope you have the pictures," Meyer called to her. "Otherwise your friend here is going to lose some important pieces."

"You cut him you don't get the pictures," she replied, spitting out foul water as it slopped over her lips.

She swam the final few yards to the yacht and used the rope ladder to climb aboard. Enzo and two other men trained their rifles on her. She had the knife between her teeth.

"I suggest you drop the knife," the big Italian said.

She did as she was told, and raised her arms.

"You stupid bitch," Meyer spat at her, coming up to slap her across the face. "You killed four of my men!"

"Four *more* of your men," she corrected him, ignoring the pain in her face. It hurt against her numb skin, but she wasn't about to give him the satisfaction. He responded by grabbing her wounded arm and sinking his fat fingers into the gash. Her blood pumped over his fingers. It hurt like fuck but she simply stood and stared him down.

He dug his nails in deeper.

She bit down on the inside of her lip hard enough to draw more blood, and as he squeezed again. She spat blood in his face.

The fat man recoiled, relinquishing his grip.

Orla reached up and undid the straps holding her tank and let it drop to the deck.

She stared at him.

He stared back.

Could he see the madness in her eyes?

Could he tell that she was done? That she didn't care if she died here, now, as long as he died right along with her?

This was when people like her were at their most dangerous, when there was nothing left to live for and everything to die for.

"Fuck you!" Meyer rasped, backing up a step. "Give me the camera." He held out his hand. It trembled with pent up rage coursing through his system. "I'll kill him," he said, grabbing Jude again.

"No you won't," she said. "Not if you want the photos." She judged the distance between them. The temptation was to move a single step and break Meyer's wrist with a savage twist. In the aftermath she could do some serious damage to his face. "I give you the camera, you let him go."

He nodded.

She handed over the camera.

"Thank you, Ms Nyrén. As promised, I will let your friend go."

And with that, he withdrew the knife and shoved Lethe in the chest so hard he staggered back against the railing and pitched over it with a desperate cry.

The sea claimed him.

SIXTEEN

They stopped her from going in after him. Enzo grabbed one arm but the other guy took the full force of her fist in his face, rupturing his nose in the process. Enzo grabbed her other arm pinning her.

"Let me go!" Orla yelled. Jude trod water out there, miles from the shore. He didn't have his tank or his BCD and it was an impossibly long way back to dry land.

"Get him out of there!"

"No," Meyer said coldly. He waved his hand dismissively. "Now we sail."

"No! You can't just leave him."

Enzo wouldn't let her go.

Orla's foot slipped on the wet deck. She dropped to one knee, her arm twisting painfully in Enzo's grip.

She stared up at him.

"Please," she said.

Enzo glanced from Orla to Meyer and back again. He wasn't going to help.

"He has a chance," Meyer said, "It isn't so far to swim back to the mouth of the Nile."

Orla kicked out at the guard whose nose she'd already ruptured, driving her foot up between his legs. He went down in agony. Enzo pinned her arms back as she kicked out. She couldn't break his grasp.

Meyer took a pistol from his belt and moved forward, aiming it at Orla's head.

It was Orla's own Jericho.

"My patience is wearing thin. I didn't have to bring you here, I don't have to keep you around. I have the photos. I have the timbers. I have the disc. There is nothing I need you for. The more you go out of your way to piss me off, the more likely I am to pull the trigger. Do you think I needed you down there? Any one of my people could have found that statue. You have no special gift."

The same thing had been bugging her ever since she'd woken up as his prisoner. He had everything he wanted. There was nothing she could add to the equation he didn't already have. Nothing that he couldn't get from anyone else, anyway. It didn't make sense that he had brought her here, or made her dive. What wasn't she seeing?

"Siegfried, have Roberto get us out of here. I'm fed up of having the horizon always moving."

The guard hurried away to the front of the boat.

"You need him," Orla insisted. "Listen to me. He's a genius. He can put your star charts together for you. He can decipher the entire thing faster than anyone you've got. Don't be a dick about this, bring him in."

"Enzo!" Meyer said, "Take Ms Nyrén down below and lock her up."

The big man hesitated, looking out to where Jude seemed to have stopped struggling.

He was going under.

"Enzo!" Meyer said again, "I will not repeat myself."

The giant let go of Orla and dived into the water. She would have followed, but one of the other men put a gun to her head and restrained her arm. Cutting through the surf with powerful strokes, it took him only a few seconds to reach Jude. He hooked his arms around the struggling man, tilting his head back so that his mouth was clear of the water. Then the big man dragged Jude back to the boat.

The handful of remaining guards scattered to make way as Enzo heaved Jude up onto the deck. Meyer could barely contain his fury.

Orla ignored Meyer and crawled on her hands and knees to where Jude lay on his stomach. He coughed up three mouthfuls of water that spread in a vomit-like pool beside his head and lay still.

"He would not have sunk," Enzo panted his explanation to Meyer. "We only draw attention to ourselves if we leave body behind. He must come with us, dead or alive. It is the only thing that makes sense. I will not go to jail for you, Mister Adler. Not for something so stupid."

The fat man's disgust was clear. He clenched and unclenched his fists over and over again, burning up with impotent rage. Finally, he stalked away.

Jude opened his eyes.

More seawater dribbled from his lips. He drew his legs up into the foetal position. He wiped his face. "I'm never leaving Nonesuch again."

Enzo helped him stand.

Orla took Jude by the arm. "You okay to walk?"

"Yeah," he lied, his voice shaking. His knees buckled and he would have fallen if not for Enzo.

"Move!" one of Meyer's men snapped, waving his rifle at them. "Downstairs now!"

Supporting Jude between them, Orla and Enzo shuffled across the deck to the stairs.

"Thank you," Orla said.

"No problem. Can't let the little man drown."

Enzo took them to the cabin, a few moments later, the door opened again and Siegfried stumbled inside. The door slammed and locked behind him.

"This is the worst vacation ever," Jude said.

She managed a laugh. "No argument there."

"Adler has all the pieces now. It is only a matter of time before he finds the Fleece."

Orla began stripping off her wetsuit.

She wore only her underwear on underneath, Siegfried turned his back. Orla didn't care what the old man saw. She examined her damaged arm. It hurt like a bastard. "That's assuming it's even a real thing," she said, feeling out the wound. "Does Meyer really believe it is the key to reinstating the monarchy?"

"He believes the time is right," Siegfried replied as if that explained everything.

Orla's arm was still bleeding, though none of the gashes were too deep. She needed to stem the bleeding. "He doesn't look much like a king."

"He contends that the people of Greece are fed up with their government, with austerity, with the country being constantly on the brink of financial collapse. He is promising to make the land truly great again, a land of heroes and kings."

Orla grabbed the bedding and pulled it out from under Jude. She began tearing it into strips, some wide, some narrow. The thinner strips she wrapped around her arm. The white linen turned red in spots right away, but she continued to wrap the makeshift bandage around her arm, until the blood was no

147

longer visible through the outer layer. She tied it off and then put on her white shirt and jeans she'd been wearing when they were captured.

The door unlocked and opened.

Enzo entered with another armed man.

"Mr Meyer is asking for you Siegfried, and for you, Mr Jude, up on deck. You come with me." As Orla started to follow, Enzo shook his head. "Not you, *Bellissima*, you stay here until you are called for. Believe me, it is better that you stay." Enzo winked at her.

He closed the door behind them, leaving Orla alone in the cabin.

She heard the door lock, but then, curiously, the sound came a second time.

She waited until she was sure they were gone before she tried the door.

It opened.

"Enzo, you big beautiful bastard."

SEVENTEEN

The lower deck was deserted.

Orla searched the cabins. There was nothing that could obviously be used as a weapon. She'd have to improvise.

She'd decided what she was going to do to Meyer; Maria Petridis had given her the idea with her talk of an eye for an eye. She intended to weigh the fat man down with whatever concrete shoes she could improvise and throw him overboard. A part of her even considering wearing the SCUBA gear so she could swim down and watch him drown. It wasn't about enjoyment, it was about justice, and that would be justice.

For now she had to make do with a cast iron skillet from the galley. Meyer would no doubt be mortified at the idea of a woman taking out his elite force with a frying pan. Orla crept up the narrow flight of stairs and paused at the hatch. She could see Meyer, Siegfried and Lethe gathered around a low table. They were flanked by Enzo and three more of Meyer's steroid addled brutes. The goons actively looked away, making a point of not watching what they were doing. Enzo was different. He watched it all. It was reasonable to assume those four were all that remained of Meyer's forces. The only other person on the boat would be the skipper, so five. She ran through a series of scenarios where she took out one or more of them, playing out what happened next in her head and trying to calculate the best chances of Jude's survival.

Right now doing nothing was the most obvious way he kept breathing, so she remained hidden on the stairs. Patience was part of the game. She'd heard Noah talk about waiting five days for a single shot when he was out in Afghanistan. She wasn't quite that patient, but then she wasn't a shooter. He was.

Eventually someone would come for her and she'd play Ten Little Indians with her shipmates.

"This just doesn't *work*," Jude objected. "Look at them. Were they drawn up on a different planet? Nothing aligns."

"Not with the modern constellations, no," Siegfried agreed. "But thousands of years ago this might as well have been a different planet. From this latitude none of the stars in our sky look the same as they did then."

Lethe nodded. "Makes sense. So what we need is a way to map the star chart into the sky we see now?"

"On the contrary, remember we are not looking for a location somewhere out in the universe. We are looking for a map that corresponds very specifically with somewhere here on Earth."

"We need processing power. We can't work this out without the right software."

"Don't think for a moment I will be stupid enough to let you play with your toys, Mr Lethe. I am not about to let you call down an air strike." His lips twisted in something approximating grin. He was one angry man.

"Siegfried, fetch the laptop. Enzo, fetch the woman."

Orla descended the stairs quickly and ducked into her cabin.

Enzo entered, alone.

"I left the door unlocked for you," he said, seemingly hurt that she was still there.

"I know. I need weapon. All I found was this." She indicated the frying pan and mimed braining Meyer with it.

Enzo laughed. "You are too much, *Bellissima*."

"You need to take me upstairs."

He nodded. "We pretend I am your guard."

"I like the sound of that. Where's bellezza?"

"You remembered?" Enzo drew the gun.

"Of course. You have to be convincing."

"Yes." Enzo nodded and pointed the gun at her. "Let's do this."

Orla opened the door.

She didn't see the fist before it crashed into her face. She stumbled backwards, knocking Enzo down.

"You treacherous bastard!" Meyer screamed.

He followed his two men into the room.

All three were armed.

"I bring her to you," Enzo protested, offering a hand to help Orla up.

She took it, and rose, feeling out her jaw gingerly.

"I heard the pair of you laughing, moron! After your Superman act to save the skinny bastard it was obvious you couldn't be trusted. So the bitch turned your head eh? What did she do, blow you?"

Enzo shrugged. "What can I say? I am weak for beauty."

"Then your cock just got you killed," Meyer raised his gun and shot Enzo in the chest.

The big man went down, his face contorted in pain and shock.

Orla crouched down beside him, trying to stem the flow of blood from the wound. She pressed hard, but the blood spilled through her fingers with each weakening beat of his heart. There was nothing she could do for him. She knew it and he knew it. She knelt over him. He looked up at her. "There are... worse places to die than... in your arms... *Bellissima*." He reached for her hand, his once strong grip now feeble.

And then he was gone.

Meyer sat down on the cabin's only chair and rested Orla's Jericho on the arm.

She looked at the weapon.

She looked at him.

Meyer shook his head.

He produced a cigar, a grotesque Cuban phallic substitute, from his pocket and cut the end off with a silver clipper. "Sit," he said, almost reasonably.

Orla laid Enzo out on the floor and stood up.

She moved back to the bed, her one ally in this mess gone.

Orla sat across from Adler Meyer as the fat man struck a match to light the cigar. Adler puffed a few times on the end theatrically before turning his attention to her. "I genuinely can't believe how stupid you are, woman," he said, exhaling a veil of smoke. "Death follows you everywhere. You are a plague."

"And you are the walking dead," Orla said, her voice soft, reasonable, normal. It was always more menacing to simply be normal when you promised death. She'd learned that from the big Russian, Konstantin Khavin, who was quite capable of stripping naked to beat someone to death simply because it was practical. It's easier to wash blood off the skin than it is to get it out of a suit. He'd been scrubbing his hands with antiseptic soap when he'd explained the logic to her and it was the matter of fact nature of his explanation that chilled her, not the act itself. That was something she'd always remember, like the fact that where he came from, death came at three o'clock in the morning in the shape of the secret police kicking down the door.

Meyer stared quietly for a few seconds while he considered her answer. "You think a lot of yourself."

"I'm looking forward to killing you," she said.

"Ah, my dear, you won't live long enough. Indeed, it's almost a shame you won't see me rule the country."

Orla couldn't contain her laughter. Meyer stared contemptuously at her.

"It is my birthright."

"You don't half talk some tosh," she said. "Like a fleece is going to grant you the power to bring down governments and bend the will of armies. You're deluded."

Meyer told one of the two men with him, "Bring me Siegfried."

The guard backed out of the door and disappeared.

She could have killed him then, barehanded. She didn't need a weapon to end the fat man's life. But with the distance between the fat man and his guard, even with the gun on the arm of his chair, there was no good way to fight them both. She wasn't in a comic book. She wasn't a superhero. Either she went hard into one and risked being shot in the moment she disabled him by the other, or she wound up caught in the no man's land between them. She needed the guard to come closer, ideally to stand behind his boss, or she needed more space between them, so that she had the chance to snatch up the Jericho and change the dynamic of the killing.

He stared her down, his fingers resting a few inches from the gun.

It was a clear power play.

Neither said a word.

The silence was interrupted by a gull's mournful cry.

The guard returned, steering the older man by the elbow. It was obvious he was sick. She couldn't believe she hadn't noticed it before. Meyer enjoyed seeing his friend so submissive.

"Well my old friend, where is my treasure?"

"I don't know, not yet."

He shook his head. Nothing was going to wipe that smile off his pink lips. "You are a terrible old queen," Meyer pushed himself up out of his chair. "I know you, remember that. I know just how smart you are. I know that with all of the pieces at your fingertips the answer is right there for you to see, and yet you pretend that you cannot solve it? Sad."

Siegfried shook his head. "It is not that simple. We need time, Adler. That boy is clever. Much brighter than me, but even so, this takes time."

"You will bring me the head of John the Baptist," Meyer said, jabbing the cigar at Siegfried's face with a brutal laugh.

"You are not thinking clearly. Decoding ancient messages takes care and attention. With something like this the merest fraction of a miscalculation could see us in the middle of the Sahara. You need to let us work."

"You're holding something back. I can tell you are. Talk."

Orla said to Siegfried, "He'll threaten to kill you again in a moment," deliberately goading Meyer. She needed him to snap. "That's his go-to threat. I don't think he understands the idea of escalation. You start with something basic, like I'll hurt you, then you move up to promising permanent physical damage, stuff that goes beyond pain, and then you threaten to hurt someone close, then it's everyone they love. You don't go straight into threats of death because then there's nothing else left to promise."

Meyer launched himself at Orla, grabbing her face in his clammy hand and squeezing his fingers viciously, twisting her cheeks and lips. "You will shut the fuck up, whore." Meyer leaned in close, pressing his forehead up against hers, flecks of spittle wetting her lips. "Or I will cut your tongue out. Is that better? Or perhaps I should promise to reach in through your chest and crush your little black heart?"

Meyer shoved her to the floor.

"Better," Orla said. "But still not menacing. You come across like a petulant schoolyard bully. A big fat manchild."

The fat man laughed and turned away.

Orla seized her chance.

Her hand snaked out, reaching under Enzo's limp body for the gun tucked into his belt. She slid it free and...

He turned, finally, a sadistic smile plastered on his face. "I have one last thing for you to do—" He never got to finish the thought. Orla pulled the trigger, punctuating the fat man's final sentence for him. It wasn't anywhere near as poetic as watching him drown, or as satisfying as a watery demise would have been, but there was something about seeing the bones splinter as the bullet forced its way out through the back of his skull, opening a huge exit wound the size of her fist.

Adler Meyer's blood was everywhere.

The guard was too slow to react. Stunned by the sudden shocking violence that ended his boss, he simply gaped. Orla turned the gun on the guard and fired again, the hammer falling on an empty chamber.

Click.

She tried again, twice, three times.

One bullet.

The guard finally grasped the fact that her gun was empty, and swung his own weapon around to cut her in half with a short burst of fire.

Siegfried saved her life.

The old man grabbed at the barrel, the impact sending the spray of bullets wide of the mark. The cases spat out the top of the weapon, and then it stuttered into silence, jamming. He couldn't clear the jam before she got to him.

Orla's fist crashed into the guard's jaw and he staggered backwards, crashing through the thin wooden door. He stumbled out into the corridor, staring down at the useless weapon in his hands. Orla didn't chase him. She retrieved her Jericho from Meyer before she strode out into the corridor.

He was at the stairs, looking back.

"Nowhere left to run," she said, and pulled the trigger, putting the bullet into the base of his spine.

It didn't kill him immediately, but even if he didn't die here he'd never walk again.

Orla didn't wait for Siegfried.

After the gunshots, all bets were off. There was a single guard she knew of, keeping watch over Lethe up top.

There was no way he hadn't heard the guns going off. She hadn't heard a retaliatory shot from above, so could only pray he hadn't taken matters into his own hands and executed Jude, but rather assumed the fat man was letting his temper get the better of him. Again. It was the one positive about a volatile character running the show.

She emerged from the stairway to the sight of Jude hunched over maps on the table. She nestled the Jericho into the waistband of her jeans, the grip pushing up against the small of her back.

Meyer's last guard stood without his gun, two women either side of him, both armed.

Maria Petridis sat at the table beside Lethe.

She stood as Orla approached.

Orla scanned the deck. It was just the six of them, including Siegfried puffing his way up the steps behind her. She noted the smaller boat, built for speed, tethered alongside Meyer's yacht.

"I assume you've taken care of our mutual *friend*," Maria Petridis said, a curious emphasis on the last word. "My girls have replaced the captain, and relieved this gentleman of his weapon. Meyer has a lot of hired thugs. There seems to be precious few of them here, though. Your doing?"

"Most of them," Orla replied.

Petridis nodded "Mr Lethe here has been telling me all about the star charts you discovered, and how he's merged them to form a map. It really is most impressive."

"You okay, Jude?" Orla asked.

He nodded. He looked at her properly for the first time. He didn't mention the blood. He knew it wasn't hers, that was all that mattered in the grand scheme of things.

Meyer was dead and the last of his men disarmed.

So why did Orla still feel uneasy?

Something about this seemingly miraculous rescue just felt *off.*

She didn't trust Petridis as far as she could throw her, and that included overboard.

Maria looked over Orla's shoulder. "Ah, Siegfried, so nice of you to join us."

"You?" the thin man said, every breath he took laboured now.

"Indeed, me. Now, my old friend, perhaps you could enlighten me. Did you know Meyer intended to murder my son?" There was a ruthless quality in the way she spoke. It had that same coldness that chilled her when Konstantin stated the facts as to why he believed the victim in front of him deserved to meet their maker. If it was revenge, she already had it. Meyer was dead.

"Maria, you have to believe me. I had no idea. I couldn't believe... I couldn't accept... You *must* believe me, I loved Ares with all my heart."

Maria Petridis said nothing, but it was obvious she didn't *have* to believe him at all.

"Siegfried saved my life," Orla said.

"Did he now?"

Siegfried nodded. "I hated him. I hated him for what he did to Ares, you have to—"

"I don't have to believe you, old friend, but I can *choose* to. And I choose to believe you. So you can live."

"Thank you," Siegfried said. It seemed lacking.

Maria sat down with Jude again.

"So, clever man, and believe me since my son died I've encountered precious few *clever men*, what does this miraculous star chart tell us?"

Jude was in his element. "The first challenge was to assemble the three aspects of the triptych, which was pretty straightforward once I grasped the nature of the constellation. It's genuinely ingenious, to be honest. Like a Rubik's cube only about three-thousand years older, see?" He manipulated the images he'd transcribed from the three relics, showing how the constellation came together and exploded depending upon how precisely the parts were aligned. "There's very little margin of error."

"Mmm, yes," Maria said. She seemed vaguely amused by Jude's enthusiasm for the subject.

Something wasn't right here.

Orla was absolutely sure of it now.

And it wasn't just that she was still wired from fighting for her life. This wasn't the adrenalin comedown either.

She watched Petridis.

"Then, much more challenging, is the transfer from heaven to earth. There was to be a terrestrial link. The legends say that the Argo was taken up into the heavens, but that can't *literally* be true. So, if the star chart isn't really a map of the heavens, it *must* be a map of something much more down to Earth. Or," and here he grinned, "more specifically, *under* it."

"You really are a clever boy aren't you?" Maria Petridis said.

"Jude," Orla warned, keeping her eyes locked on Maria's two bodyguards.

"The thing is, I used deep ground penetrating radar back in Peru last month and something about the star chart reminded me of the patterns I saw in the rock."

"Did it now?"

"I brought up a geological survey of Greece," he said, smiling. "And I found it."

"Found what, exactly?"

Now his grin was huge, Cheshire-Cat-getting-the-cream wide. "The location of the Golden Fleece, of course. That's what all this is about. And I know where it is."

Maria laughed delightedly, then reached out and stroked the back of Jude's neck. It was a curiously, uncomfortably intimate gesture.

Jude didn't seem to notice it.

"Jude," Orla said, deciding there was nothing to be lost by a bit of honesty. "I don't think you should say anything else."

"Why ever not, dear Orla?" Petridis said. "We are family, after all."

"No we aren't," she said.

Maria moved away from the table and the maps spread out across it, and came over to her. The older woman took both her hands in hers. "Come, look, see for yourself what he has found."

Jude had matched the star chart to a series of underground tunnels in Crete.

"So that's it then," Orla said. "We're done. I killed Meyer for murdering Ares, the reckoning you needed, and now you have the location of the Golden Fleece. It's all over. We need to head back to shore, then we can get the next flight out of here. I just want to go home now."

"I don't think so, my dear," Maria said. Her tone was sing-song light, but there was an undercurrent of something else beneath it. "You might want to sit down for the next part." The older woman carefully teased thin flesh-coloured gloves from her hands, gloves so thin Orla hadn't realised Maria had been wearing them at all. "Contact poison. You can never be too careful."

Orla struggled to focus. She tried to reach around her back for the Jericho, but couldn't make her hands do what she wanted them to do. She couldn't think. Her mind swam along with her vision.

She saw Jude hunched over the keyboard.

A tingling sensation spread through her hands, up her arms.

Maria Petridis was suddenly so far away. So very, very far away.

The world spun, and then it was black.

EIGHTEEN

The air was heavy with the putrid smell of rotting flesh and wet leaves.

The muffled high-pitched moans – oddly reminiscent of the mating call of a humpback whale – could be heard somewhere far off.

The lighting was dim, but she wasn't in total darkness.

Weary and still in the fug of sedation, Orla struggled to control her hand enough to wipe the spittle from her face, but her arm refused to obey her for more than half a second before it fell. She tried to roll to her side, only to realise she was already prone. The dark soil was close to her face, granules snorted up her nostrils as she breathed.

She rolled awkwardly onto her back.

She willed her eyes to focus on the ceiling.

Curiously shaped stalactites dripped down towards her, stony nails on a torture chamber door waiting to slam closed.

She was in a cave.

She lay there, counting to ten. Then ten again. A third time running over the same numbers before she struggled into the sitting position.

She could see thanks to a small amount of light coming in through a crack in the ceiling. Climbing up wasn't an option.

Yet. Her side hurt. There was fresh bruising. Did the fall account for that? Had Petridis's women bundled her through the crack in the ceiling and let her fall down here?

She scanned what she could see of the cavern, looking for an alternative way out.

It was hard to see much beyond her immediate surroundings.

But the fact that the cavern felt like a tomb – her own personal grave – was unmistakable. Where was she? Crete, she thought, remembering Lethe's excitement. Again she heard a weird *baying* sound off in the darkness. It sounded like an artificial alarm but somehow being reproduced by a real voice?

It was still far off.

She blinked away the dust that still filmed her eyes, trying to focus in the gloom.

A harrowing scream burst through the air, filling cavern and echoing all around her, only getting louder as it bounced off the moist walls. It was primeval. Whoever made that scream was fighting for his life.

Jude.

Orla's head pounded to the rhythm of her heart.

Trying to concentrate on something – anything other than the pain, she looked down at her once-white shirt, now filthy with a combination of Enzo's blood, water and soil. Her shoes were missing, but otherwise she was fully clothed. A tear in her jeans exposed a scraped and bloodied kneecap.

The lingering effect of the drug enticed her to lapse back into oblivion, but she fought to concentrate and stay at least partially alert. How many hours – days even – had she been out? She shook her head and sniffed.

The foul smell lingered on the air.

Her bandaged forearm was aching, which was a good sign.

The sweat from her forehead trickled down her temples and she clumsily wiped it away. She lay in the muddy pile of leaves until another sharp cry pierced the darkness. She listened for any sign of advancing footsteps.

Orla shook herself, slapped her face three times in quick succession, trying to smack some life back into her sluggish body.

Another terrible scream echoed through the cavernous space.

It sounded so much closer than before.

She couldn't tell if it was Jude. She prayed it wasn't, feared it was.

Placing her hand against the cave wall she gingerly negotiated the bed of stalagmites until she reached a small tunnel opening in the cavern wall. Cautiously, she stepped through, searching the walls for surveillance cameras or anything to indicate that she was being watched.

There was nothing.

She followed the tunnel as it curved away, noting the shallow decline as the pathway curled around a blind turn. Ten metres on it had dropped maybe half a metre. The walls were covered with bright spots; they helped light the way.

Orla examined one, surprised to see it wriggle.

The walls were lined with glow worms. Thousands of them, writhing and wriggling, cast their eerie bluish light. She'd never been so grateful for something so freakish. They saved her from being alone in the dark.

Another twenty metres on she found another opening in the wall.

She peered in, trying to adjust her eyes to the gloom of the new cave.

Without the benefit of the living light sources, it took a moment for her eyes adjust enough to determine that the second smaller cave was empty. Orla returned to the tunnel. She kept moving downwards, following the curve. The next cave mouth was closer. She saw the slumped shape of a person huddled up against the far wall. It was Jude, curled up pitifully, like a broken bird, all twisted up against the cold wall of the cavern. A spasm of guilt punched Orla's gut. She was responsible for his being here. He'd come to help her. The rabbit-hole plunged deeper than she had imagined.

A pool of light illuminated the middle of the cavern, again streaming down through a skylight much like the one she'd woken beneath, meaning there were multiple points of entry into the cavern complex.

She crouched down over him, and stroked the side of his face, attempting to revive him. It was only then that she noticed how muddied her hands were. They left a pattern like clover on his cheek.

Her palms were bleeding.

She wiped her hands on her jeans and when she looked back to Jude, he was gazing up at her. "I'm all holidayed out," he said wearily.

She forced a smile. "Agreed. No more holidays."

"Where the fuck are we?" he asked as she helped him sit up.

"Underground. Somewhere. And I'm not sure we're alone. I heard something howling. At least I think it was howling. I'm just glad it wasn't you."

"It smells like death down here," he said.

"You know, if I wanted to die, I could have stayed at Nonesuch and tried to teach the old man to code."

"Consider yourself lucky."

"How did we even get here? The last thing I remember was Mamma Ares stroking the back of my neck very inappropriately."

"She was wearing gloves soaked in some sort of contact poison, potent enough to work on skin contact, but non-lethal. We must have been out a long time for them to get us to Crete."

"Crete? How do you know we're in Crete?"

"You told her this was where the pot of gold was waiting."

"Right, the star chart mapping to a geological survey of underground tunnels in Crete. Me and my big mouth. We must have been dumped down here for a reason."

"To rot," Orla said as another cry pierced the darkness, raising the fine hairs on the back of her neck.

"What was *that*?" Lethe shuddered.

"That was our company down here."

"Oh, it just keeps getting better. Tell me there aren't any nukes down here."

"Pretty sure we're good on that score. Can you walk?" He nodded begrudgingly. "Good, because we've got to get moving."

They stood, using the walls of the cave for support, and made their way to the cavern's entrance.

"What the hell was that screaming about?"

"I don't even want to think about it."

Cautiously, they followed the passage.

Again they came upon another cavern, this one empty. Some of the caverns had a pool of light in the centre from a skylight. More entry points. They found two more empty rooms, these without skylights. It wasn't until they reached a sixth cavern that they found another living soul: a shape huddled at the back, barely discernable from the thicker shadow, not moving.

"Hello?" Orla whispered. "Hello?" she repeated, edging along the wall.

The lump shifted, its black colour shiny and wet in the little light provided by the worms.

She reached down, her hand on the curve of the lump's back. It rolled beneath her touch, revealing a man with half his face torn off. She saw ragged wound where huge teeth had ripped through his throat.

"He's dead," Orla said.

"I should hope so, he's only got half a face."

"Whatever did this to him is still close."

She recognised the corpse. It was the last of Meyer's men.

"Poor bastard."

Judging by the bite marks, they were looking at something smaller than a wolf, bigger than a coyote. She didn't say anything.

Jude followed her as she left the cavern, captivated by the glow worms illuminating the walls. They walked on in silence, stopping as they heard more baying, uncomfortably close.

"Is it getting darker?"

Orla hadn't wanted to admit it, but as they descended, the density of glowworms had dropped steadily. She could no longer see her feet, and visibility was down to a few metres ahead.

"What's the noise?" Jude asked. "It's like insects or something? It sounds close."

"Stop!"

"Oh Christ, something just brushed past my foot!"

Orla felt something moving down there.

She couldn't see a thing.

She plucked glow worms from the walls, allowing them to crawl over her hands and forearms. She scooped up as many of them as she could. Jude did the same. The bugs crawled over their flesh.

Orla crouched down, lowering her arms towards the ground.

Jude gasped.

Snakes.

NINETEEN

The floor was covered with writhing serpents.

Raising her glowing arm, Orla saw them covering the ground all the way down the tunnel, coiled around each other, over each other, to form a living, venomous carpet.

They had no choice but to push on through them.

One coiled itself around her ankle.

"Oh Christ, oh shit, oh God. Orla get them *off* me!"

"Just relax, Jude. They won't bite you unless you give them a reason to."

"Are they poisonous?"

"Venomous."

"Are you being fucking pedantic about my word choice?"

Orla actually laughed. "It's an important distinction. We need to go on." She waved her worm-covered hands at the snakes. They recoiled from the light, slithering over each other to get out of the way. A pathway of sorts opened up for them through the snakes. "They don't like the light."

"I wish I had fire. Lots of fire."

She glanced back at Jude. "Okay, you ready?"

"Fuck no."

"Just move nice and slowly. Shuffle your feet, don't lift them. We don't want to step on one."

"Do the two-step shuffle. When we get out of here I'm applying for *Strictly*."

"Sounds perfect. I'll lead."

"You always do," he said.

Orla shuffled forward, into the carpet of snakes. The serpents responded with hisses as they recoiled from the light.

Jude copied her, two steps behind.

With every half-step he muttered a different and more inventive curse, "Shit. Fuck. Arse. Bollocks. Cunt. Christ." She smiled at the thought of Cunt Christ, and wondered who might worship such a deity.

Their progress was painfully slow, a half-step at a time, eyes always forward, surrounded by the rising hiss, a susurrant chorus that seemed to grow louder and louder the deeper they shuffled, before gradually softening and thinning. The light from the glowworms offered less and less in terms of forked tongues licking at their heels, while more and more could be seen congregating on the walls The snakes massed where there were fewer worms, shying away from their light.

"If I go first you have permission to eat me," Jude said.

"A reason to go vegetarian if ever I heard one."

They emerged into a cavernous chamber that housed a row of pillars. Each pillar, she saw, marked the start of another seemingly endless passage that curved away into darkness. They halted in the middle of the cavern, turning and turning again as they considered the selection of exits.

A labyrinth.

In Crete.

Orla stared up at the enormous pillars. They were carved out of the stone of the mountain, dating back centuries at least. "We're going to have to choose one."

"And what? Hope we don't pick the tunnel leading to something else that wants to eat us?"

"Maybe there's a Minotaur waiting down here to chow down on our bones," she said.

"Shut up."

The baying sound echoed around them, louder than before.

Orla stood still, trying to determine which corridor it was coming from. The weird acoustics of the cavern confused her ears, making the cries come from every direction at once. Her skin crawled.

They were coming closer, searching them out.

"There's a breeze coming from this one." Jude pointed to the tunnel on the right.

"This one smells rotten," Orla said, sniffing at the left tunnel. "It smells like death."

"Then I'm all for right," Jude said.

Orla held him back.

"We need to be careful," she warned. "We don't know anything about this maze. There's a good chance there's *no* exit. Open pits? Deadfalls filled with stakes?"

As the animals drew nearer, Orla could make out the howling of individual beasts. A pack. Hunting.

"Jude," Orla warned.

"I'm trying to remember. It's starting to feel familiar."

"From the survey? How can you possibly remember that?"

"It's the way my brain works," he said. "It's about patterns. This place is laid out in concentric circles that radiate from a central hub. The trick is we need to find the centre, then we can find a way out."

"You sure?"

She heard scurrying sounds now to accompany the howling. Claws on rock, scraping and scratching. Rats?

"This one," he said, and headed off down the right-hand tunnel. Orla hurried after him. She could hear them out there in the darkness, stalking there. The rasp of their breathing. The shallow *pant, pant, pant.* They were closer and getting closer all of the time. The scratching of claws on the ground revealed them to be much bigger than rats.

There were more glow worms here than before, enough to bathe the passageway in an eerie blue light.

They reached another fork in the tunnel, which presented her with more options that she really wanted.

The air was stale.

Old.

The chill tightened her skin.

She glanced back the way they'd come, and caught a glimpse of movement in the shadows. Something *prowled* back there.

She struggled to get a good look at it; wolf-like, but smaller, more compact. She threw a handful of worms in its direction, causing the creature to growl deep in its throat, the muscles oscillating as it padded slowly towards them. The low-guttural noise filled Orla with dread.

"Is that a *wolf*?"

She shook her head. "No. A jackal," she said.

"Okay, one question: do jackals eat *people*?"

She had no idea, but it was safe to assume they'd got a taste for human flesh given the corpse they'd found near where they started. "Usually? No. But there's nothing usual about this place."

"It doesn't look... hungry."

The animal snarled at them, halting again, lowering its front end, muscles bunched, ready to pounce.

"I take that back."

Orla couldn't wait for it to strike. Once that thing charged at them the balance of the encounter would be shifted forever. She tried to think but the best she could come up with was running straight at it, screaming and yelling, waving her arms, making herself appear huge and imposing, a thing to be feared not hunted.

So that was exactly what she did.

The jackal turned tail and padded away, retreating down the passage and disappearing around the corner.

"That's the best you could come up with?" Jude said as she returned to his position.

"It worked didn't it? Which way?"

Jude stared at the branching corridor ahead.

Orla waited impatiently. "You think it's true what they say about mazes? If you put your hand on one wall and follow it without letting go, you'll get out?"

"I'd prefer access to a GPS tracker and satellite schematics."

"Google Maps would do me," she said.

"I'm not sure Streetview would be much use here."

Lethe leaned his head against the wall, working through their choices. Orla knew there were several variations on the basic design of any labyrinth. People had been building them for centuries, perfecting them to the point of bamboozlement. But certain basic tenets of these structures were almost universal.

At last Jude lifted his head and spoke. "Have you noticed that the further we go the more the tunnel's floor slopes downwards?" She nodded. "I'm thinking we follow the tunnels with the steepest gradient. Anything that appears flat, discount, anything seeming to rise, we ignore. I know it's counter intuitive to think about going deeper, but I think the key is to find our way to the bottom of the pit, not the top. I don't think there's a way out up there."

"Big risk," Orla said.

"Not really," he disagreed. "You're trying to fuck with people's minds, what better way than to make down up and up down, at least logically? You're underground, you believe going up will bring you back to the surface. It transforms it into an impossible maze if you're always looking in the wrong place for the way out."

"I can buy that," Orla agreed. "Okay, you take left, I'll take right. First one to find the way down, shout."

They set off along separate branches of the network of tunnels.

Half a minute later she was sure hers was ascending, it was gradual, but noticeable. Jude confirmed it a few seconds later, calling out, "Mine goes down!" His words echoed weirdly, folding back on themselves. She started back to his position. "I've found someone."

She retraced her step to the fork in the passageway, but was blocked from going any further.

A dozen jackals waited for her.

The species wasn't indigenous to Crete, which meant that someone had brought them here from the mainland, perhaps centuries ago, and ever since they'd been living down here in the dark, feeding on snakes and rodents and anything else that stumbled into their lair. Making noise and running at them might have frightened a lone animal away, but a whole pack?

"Look who I found," Jude said, approaching from the other tunnel.

He wasn't alone.

Siegfried was with him, obviously in some discomfort, skin pallid and clammy even under the dim glow of the worms.

Orla put a finger to her lips and pointed towards the pack of jackals, before Jude could say anything more. The animals crept closer, wary but emboldened by the promise of fresh meat. But still they held back as though waiting for something.

Siegfried froze. "Golden jackals," the old man said, reverentially. "I haven't seen their like *years*. And never on the island."

"They might have been living down here for centuries," Orla said. "Since this labyrinth was constructed."

"Guardians of the Fleece," Siegfried said. "Golden ones to guard the Golden Fleece."

"Perhaps."

"We can't run, they'll give chase," Orla said. "We need to head down your tunnel."

The old man shook his head. "It's a dead end. I've been all the way to the bottom. I thought there was a door, I saw a small indentation there, something that might act as a setting, but I couldn't see the outline of a door, or a break in the stonework."

"Take us to it," Orla said.

They edged down the passage, always glancing back over their shoulders as the jackals followed. The creatures sniffed the chill air, pawing the ground. Their growls hummed in the eerie glowworm light, deep and full of threat. They were getting braver. It was only a matter of time before they pounced.

Two more jackals arrived. One of them carried something in its mouth.

"That's a human bone," said Orla. "I think." A thigh bone by the look of it. The new arrival clearly had rank amid the pack, its alpha. It had been feasting on Meyer's man.

That was what the pack had been waiting for, their leader.

He dropped the bone.

One of the others snatched it up and hurried away to crunch through to the marrow and feast. Two more chased after him.

The leader advanced, jowls slick with saliva and blood.

The beast held no trace of fear.

"Forget everything I said. *Go go go,*" Orla barked.

They didn't hesitate. They ran, as best they could.

Siegfried managed no more than fifteen metres before he pulled up short, shaking his head.

The jackals weren't running. They had infinite patience. They knew their quarry couldn't escape. They knew the tunnels.

The jackals blocked their escape.

They growled and butted each other, jostling for position behind their leader.

They all wanted a feed.

"You two go," Siegfried said. "I'm dying. What difference is it if I go now or in two months? I am done. You go. I will buy you time, not much I fear, there's not so much meat on these old bones. Work out how to open the door." He looked at Jude in the eerie light. "You can do it. Your mind is sharper than mine. Perhaps doing this will make amends for my failure to protect young Ares? I shall find out, if I enter Elysium or find myself deeper in the pits of Tartarus with Hades mocking me for my pitiful sacrifice."

"We're not leaving you," Orla said.

"It is my life to spend, go."

Jude put a hand on Orla's shoulder. "He's right," he said. "And arguing is just wasting time. It's his life. Don't diminish his sacrifice by trying to talk him out of it."

"The boy is wise," the old man said. "Fare thee well."

"Thank you, for everything," she said, not knowing what else to say.

"You are very welcome."

She grabbed Jude and propelled him along the tunnel, forcing him to run, first pushing and then dragging him along behind her. She didn't slow down. She didn't look back. She didn't think about what was happening back there.

They reached the end of the tunnel less than a minute later.

Lethe put his hands flat against the wall blocking the passage, feeling out the stone until he found the recessed hole. It could easily be a random depression in the rock. Orla felt around for more cracks, or a seam running through the stone. The old man was right, there was no sign of any hidden door.

Behind them came the sickening sound of the pack *baying* and the single shrill scream of the old man, cut short by death.

The echo of the jackals feasting filled the tunnel.

Orla returned to the wall, focussing on the task at hand. She was calm. Centred. The wall presented a challenge. She put her hand into the indentation. It was circular, about a centimeter deep, and maybe fifteen in diameter. She felt granular little impressions inside it, like a message hidden in braille, which reminded her of the disc hanging nestled between her breasts.

Had he given it to her because he knew, ultimately, it would save her life?

The sound of the jackals grew louder. They'd stripped the old man down to bones and were ready for their next meal. She and Jude had seconds.

Orla removed her necklace and placed the Phaistos Disc into the indentation, rotating it slightly until the indentations of the star chart fell into place and it slotted in snugly, a perfect fit.

There was a distinct *thunk* of gears turning over and tumblers dropping, deep and resonant, emanating from within the stone. Orla hauled Lethe in close as the first of the jackals rounded the last corner. It inclined its head, looking at them, then moved forward, head down, prowling towards them.

The ground beneath their feet shifted.

It took her a moment to grasp what was happened, as the dais they stood on rolled, the entire section of wall rotated. It wasn't fast enough, and the jackal sensed its prey about to be snatched away from under its nose and launched itself. Orla didn't think twice, she clenched her first and drove a sledgehammer punch into its snout, enraging the animal even as it skittered away, claws scratching at the stone floor.

And then it was gone, or more accurately they were gone, the dais completed its revolution and the wall sealed up behind them.

There were bones scattered across the ground, including a picked bare skull. All human, at least as far as she could tell. The ground appeared to be littered with them.

"I'm guessing they're set decoration?" Jude said, hopefully.

Orla said nothing. She was quietly mourning the loss of the necklace, the Phaistos Disc copy Ares had given her. When the dais had rotated, the disc, acting as a key, remained on the other side, out of reach. She surprised herself by how much it hurt to lose it.

Returning to the present, Orla collected the few remaining worms that still clung to their feet and ankles. It wasn't much in the way of illumination, but it was better than complete darkness. There was enough light to see more of the skeletal remains littered across the floor. It was impossible to judge the actual size of the cavernous chamber, but it was big.

They moved away from the door.

"Are we looking for something other than a way out?" Jude asked, his feet crunching on brittle bones.

"Well, if we trip over a ram's fleece spun from gold I figure we take it with us as souvenir."

"Sounds reasonable."

Orla saw the tripwire an instant before Jude triggered it.

She was too late to warn him.

She didn't hesitate: she hit the ground, dragging Jude down with her.

He knew better than to argue.

She felt rather than heard the rumbling deep beneath their feet.

The cavern shook so violently it could only mean the walls were coming down, surely?

She was dimly aware of something scything past over their heads. When it returned seconds later, travelling in the other direction, Orla realised what it was: a gigantic double-headed axe, the blades easily twice the size of her own skull.

Still the ground shook.

The blade swung over their heads again, its arc diminishing with each pass until it lay still.

It wasn't the end of it.

Orla cast about desperately for an exit, but it was still far too dark to see much beyond the bones shaking at their feet and the blade hanging over their heads.

And then the ground fell away.

So did the ceiling.

Orla scrambled back, her hand clamped around Jude's wrist and his around hers as a pit opened up. The only thing that saved them was that they hadn't ventured deeply enough into the cavern. The rim of the pit ran around the edge of the cavern. They were six inches from the drop, balanced precariously. She clung on to Jude, not about to let him fall, as he struggled to find safe footing.

It took a moment to register the fact that she could now see the entire width of the pit.

She could also see the silver blade of the axe hanging over them and the great chains that suspended it from the ceiling.

Dozens of small pinprick holes had opened up in the roof of the cavern, sending down needles of light. They were too narrow to offer any hope of escape, but each one penetrated so far into the rock, they punched out into sunlight. They conjured a forest of fine beams of light around them.

Orla hauled Jude back onto solid ground at the edge of the newly formed pit.

The rumbling had stopped, and with it the tremors.

Orla looked around for a way out, but even though she could see the far side of the cavern, no obvious exit presented itself.

There was, however, a single item of interest: in the centre of the pit, suspended over the seemingly bottomless drop, a wooden box hung suspended in the air.

Orla moved closer to the edge, trying to see how it could possibly just hover there without anything to hold it in place.

She moved her head so she could see the wooden chest better, trying to find a position where she wasn't staring at it through a hundred needle-fine beams of sunlight.

"It's on a plinth," she said, seeing the rock pillar that hadn't crumbled away when the pit collapsed. It was a tall, freestanding column, which appeared to maintain a constant width all the way down to vanishing point, as far as Orla could see it went on forever, all the way down to Tartarus. It was as though Nelson's Column had been dropped into a giant hole. The pit was too wide for her to be able to reach the chest, even with a running jump. There was nothing to cling onto, nowhere to land, meaning nowhere to go but down. That was more than just a leap of faith.

"You want to see what's in there, don't you?" Jude said. "What's in the box? What's in the box?" He mimicked the out-of-control Brad Pitt facing the prospect of seeing his dead wife's head grinning up at him from within John Doe's special delivery.

"Nope. I just want to get out of here."

"You're seriously going to leave it there?"

"Yup."

"You're a better woman than I am."

"No comment."

Orla circled the pit, staring up at the ceiling. None of the fissures were wide enough to climb through, so she turned her attention to the outer walls.

There had to be a way out of this hell.

Had to be.

But nothing presented itself.

"You know how I think we get out?" Jude said. "We solve the riddle. We get the Fleece."

"Fine," she said, weary. She couldn't see an alternative. "Someone really wants us to get that damned thing. It's not like ancient, overly-elaborate traps ever kill people, right?"

"So what are you thinking?"

"Might as well jump," she said.

"You can't be serious."

"Do you see an invisible platform to walk across?" He didn't say anything to that. She took his silence as all the answer she needed. "And let's be honest, no choir of angels is going to sweep down to bear us over the gap. So if you've got a better idea?"

Again, he had nothing.

She walked back a few steps, looking at the axe's blade and trying to picture the arc the chains would proscribe as she sailed out over the pit, and when—if—there'd ever be a good moment to relinquish her grip. It was nothing short of suicidal. And with that in mind, she rocked back on her heels like a long jumper, and sprinted for the edge,

She almost missed the leap, her stride too long, meaning she pushed off with too much ground before the rim, and too far to the hanging axe, but she arced out and up, bending her back and throwing her arms forward to give her momentum, and at the very last possible moment caught the top of the blade. Her grip was slightly off centre, and her weight yanked down on the chains, setting a shudder running through the links as it swung beneath her. She used her body, arching her back and swinging her legs to get some proper distance to the chain, turning herself into a pendulum.

As the blade reached the zenith of its arc, she let go.

She arced through the air, nothing beneath her, nothing above, the thousands of points of light spearing down through her as she reached out desperately for the chest, but her angles were all wrong, she was short, and gravity meant she was going to fall even shorter.

She barely reached the column, slamming bodily into it. Before she fell away, Orla jammed her hand into a fissure running deep through the stone. Her entire weight pulled down on her wrist, but she didn't fall.

She hung there for as long as it took to gather her breath and slow the rapid chase of her heart. She took a moment to centre herself before she used the hand-jam to lever herself upwards. Her feet caught on rough edges of the stonework, searching desperately for purchase. She scrabbled against the rock, and then her right foot found a couple of millimetres of lip to use as a toehold. She raised herself up, looking for another handhold before she worked her hand free of the jam.

She lifted herself up onto the platform.

The wooden chest was banded with iron. There was no lock. There were no chains. It was just a wooden chest.

Orla opened it.

She reached inside.

Something glinted in the hundreds of needles of sunlight, like a rug.

She retrieved it.

The material was coarse, but unmistakably spun from real gold.

It was *heavy* in her hands.

"Time to let us out of here," Orla told whatever gods watched over the labyrinth.

And then the column, the chest and Orla dropped away.

TWENTY

Orla fell.

The column crumbled as it collapsed, leaving just her and the wooden chest tumbling down what was rapidly turning into a sloping tunnel.

She saw Lethe behind her, trying to cling to the side of the wall, like a spider, then launching himself after her when he realised the pit wasn't bottomless.

As the column filled the ground beneath it with debris, the platform it formed levelled off, and finally she stopped falling and flailing and lay on her back, looking up at Lethe who had retrieved the Fleece.

Thick dust clouds filled the air.

She was battered and bruised, but very much alive, so those lacerations were fantastic as far as she was concerned. Her right arm, the one already bandaged from the knife cuts, hung awkwardly, a shard of bone piercing out through the skin.

It was agony to move, but she had no choice.

Lethe clambered down to her position.

"Are you okay?"

"I'll live," she said, downplaying the pain she was in. "You?"

"I think I broke a couple of ribs," he complained.

He helped her up.

On top of the searing pain in her arm, the fall had shaken her. She struggled to breathe because of all the dust in the thick cloying air. Lethe coughed, then winced, then coughed and winced some more, holding an arm pressed tight across his ribs as if he could press them in place against the muscular spasms. It didn't work. He looked at her, tears tracking the dust down his cheeks. All he could do was cough it up. She couldn't make it any easier for him.

It was gloomy down here, but not pitch black.

Some strands of light still filtered through from the steep slope they'd tumbled down.

The passageway continued ahead.

The dust gradually settled.

Orla stumbled forward, unsure if the breeze against her face was real or imaginary.

No, it was real. Air. Fresh air. It was faint, like a feather up against her skin, but it was real, and it meant the way ahead led to the outside world.

Jude felt it too. "I'm not getting my hopes up. Even hell has windows."

He still carried the fleece, and using her good arm Orla held on to him. They stumbled slowly over the rubble-strewn floor, battered, broken, but far from beaten.

More than anything she just wanted to feel the sunlight on her skin.

The tunnel grew steadily brighter as they walked.

Time meant nothing now. The world measured its passing in footsteps. Orla focussed on putting one in front of the other and repeating the process.

She hurt. The adrenalin was wearing off. Her arm was a mess.

But finally, leaning on Lethe, she stepped out into the afternoon air.

The cool breeze coming in off the water was blessed relief.

They left the cave, struggling with the rocky terrain, with no option but to head for the water.

Orla looked back. Cliffs towered above the cave they'd emerged from. Maybe once upon a time they'd been a pirate cove or the inspiration for Homer's legendary Odysseus and the gateway to Scylla and Charybdis, a choice between two evils. Because that's what it always came down to in these myths, a choice between the Meyers and Petridises of the world, with no good solution.

And as armed men swarmed their position, their submachine guns trained on the exhausted pair, Orla saw Maria Petridis walking towards them across the golden sands.

There was no point in trying to hide the artefact.

"My boy chose well," the woman said.

She carried no weapon.

She didn't need one with all of the others at her command.

She wore an elegant red dress and low-heeled sandals, footwear slightly more suitable for the rocky beach than her usual stilettos. There was no malice in her eyes. Rather, she seemed *proud*.

At Maria's signal, one of her men took the Fleece from Jude. He was far from keen to let it go, but pragmatic. It wasn't a fight they could win in their condition.

"I think I've worked you out," Orla said, looking at the matriarch of the Petridis family. Maria was just a few feet from her now. The two women stared each other down. Orla cradled her broken arm in her good one.

"Have you now?" Maria said. She looked so much like her son in this light. She shared his beauty and athleticism.

"It's time for the monarchy to be reinstated, don't you think? You could be Queen of all this and more. That must be a temptation."

"If that is what you believe, you don't have me all worked out, my dear," Maria Petridis replied. "While Adler Meyer intended to make himself king, I have no such ambitions. My place is in the shadows, it always was and always will be. Without me, my country would not be deep in the enormous financial crisis that is consuming it, but then it wouldn't have a means of escape, either. You have been here a while. You must have felt it. People are *desperate* for a new direction. A purpose. I intend to give them one. Besides," and now she did grin, "I have far too many skeletons in my closet, and business interests that skirt too closely to the flame of Russia to ever want to invite scrutiny, and I have no interest in divesting my wealth. To put it bluntly, I am too well known, and not well enough liked."

"Meyer wasn't exactly ruler material," Orla noted.

"Meyer was an idiot. He was arrogant and blind. He couldn't face up to reality. It was all some grand impossible game. He did not care what the people thought of him. Rulers in his mind have iron fists. There is no room for the love of the people. His appetite was voracious."

"I saw his gut," Orla said.

"Indeed, it is a fitting parallel. The man had no control. The monarchy as he saw it was little more than a stepping stone to greater power."

"So who would rule? Ares?"

"That was my intention, yes. But that *bastard* killed my boy. He killed Ares and broke away from AI, the company I set up to funnel money into this operation. I suspected he would but I didn't think he'd be so stupid as to murder my son."

"I can see how that might be a problem."

"I couldn't have Meyer killed personally. His death would not go down well with those who claim direct lineage to Jason. Such an overt action could well result in civil war."

"So you had me do it."

"He kidnapped you. Adler died. You escaped. It's an easy story to sell. Now I have the Fleece, an artefact Pelias ordered our last true hero to recover to prove his worth to sit upon the throne of Thessaly. It is the ultimate symbol of authority and kingship, and now I can return it to my people. It will be easy to convince them the time is right for a new Queen."

"I thought you said you didn't want to be Queen," Orla said.

"What makes you think I am talking about my personal ambitions, daughter?" Maria replied.

"I'm no child of yours," Orla said.

"On the contrary, my dear," Maria Petridis calmly withdrew a piece of paper from her handbag. She unfolded it and held it up for both of them to see. "It's a marriage certificate, witnessed and signed and perfectly legal. As far as the world knows, you married my beloved boy before his tragic death. You have suffered terribly, your love cut short by tragedy. You will be the perfect mother for my people..."

"I don't even..." was the best Orla could muster. "It's beyond insane. What the hell makes you think I'd go along with something so patently absurd, *Mother*?" Orla spat the last word, her voice laced with scorn and derision.

Maria Petridis shook her head sadly. "Must we resort to threats and violence?" It almost sounded like she regretted the prospect, save for the fact that one of her men had the needle of a hypodermic pressed up against Jude's neck. "Now, I assume you will co-operate, my dear? We are all family after all."

"I'm going to say this once, you are going to leave him the fuck alone."

"You are in no position to make demands, my girl."

"Will you stop with the my this and my that? I'm not anyone's."

Without the broken arm she would have killed the guard between her and Jude before he could loose a single shot, then made a play for the needle. It might have worked, it might not. If wishes were fishes she'd have out-catered Jesus right then and there. The reality was she didn't stand a chance.

A small bead of blood trickled from Jude's jugular.

She had no idea what was inside the syringe, or how lethal even a tiny drop of the serum was or what sort of damage exposure to it would do to Jude. She had to operate under the assumption that even the smallest amount would kill him.

She turned back to Maria. "I don't get it. There's no way you can hold him hostage long enough to pull this off. It doesn't work. Even if you crown me, then what? And what happens the day when I look at your plans and weigh them up against the life of one man and he comes up wanting? What then? Because there is always a tipping point, even with a friend. I'll kill him myself if it saves a dozen people. Willingly if it saves fifty."

"Thanks, Orla!" Jude said sarcastically.

Maria smiled benignly. "We only need to keep you around long enough for your son to grow old enough to be born."

"Small problem, I'm not fucking pregnant."

"Yet," Maria Petridis said. And this time Orla didn't like the word at all, because it promised an uncertain future, that everything could change, even if that change should be impossible. "You want to keep your friend alive, I will make you a deal, a trade, you get something you want, I get something I *need*. I have a physician waiting even now to impregnate you with my son's frozen seed. You will bear his son – don't worry we have the ability to manipulate the genetic structure of the embryo and assure it is a fit and healthy boy, after all the future of a nation depends upon him being a big strong boy. Do that, bear me a grandson, and you both go free. Nine months of your lives in return for the future of my people. It seems like a small price to claim."

"You're deluded," Orla said, struggling to grasp the full implications of the mad matriarch's words.

"All you have to do is fool the people into loving you. Look at you, you will make a fine Queen. I will be with you, one step behind you to whisper in your ear, offer you my wisdom, and I will see to it that your son will one day make the greatest ruler this country has seen since his Theseus walked this Earth."

Orla stared at her. "I don't even want to know why the fuck you have your dead son's frozen sperm, because that's just fucked up."

Maria ignored her. "First, we need to present you to the people, my dear. I have people waiting on the mainland to authenticate the Golden Fleece. You have to wear it when you are introduced to your people. The Fleece and this marriage certificate make your claim to the heritage of kings undeniable."

Orla shook her head. "It won't work."

"It will," Maria insisted, "and our great line will continue."

"It won't work. There can't be any baby."

"Nonsense."

Orla lowered her gaze to the rocks at her feet, then raised her face defiantly, ready to share the darkness of her secret self. She shook her head. "I cannot have children. Last year I was the prisoner of a vile man I called The Beast. He did things to me. Not merely torture. It went beyond abuse. I came out of that place mentally and physically damaged. I can never have children because of that monster."

"Oh Orla, I didn't know," it was Jude. He looked tormented. Like he wanted to wrap his arms around her, needle be damned. She hated the pity in his eyes.

"It was just one of the reasons I went back there and killed the bastard."

Maria Petridis stared at her. The look in her eyes was different, not sympathy, something else. Its presence was fleeting, replaced by steely resolve. "Are you sure?"

"Quite sure," Orla said. "So, like I said, no matter how twisted your scheme or brilliant your doctors, it isn't happening. You're going to need another incubator."

Maria Petridis just stood there, the wind stirring eddies in the sand around her feet, looking out over Orla's shoulder at the sea and the future that might have been, but never could.

Even now the Beast was in control of her life.

The Greek woman turned and walked away without another word, leaving Orla there on the sands. Jude was released, Maria's men left with her, taking the precious relic with them.

There was no sentimental goodbye, no moment of shared grief as they mourned the man they had both lost. For Orla Nyrén it was a single moment of purity. She existed in that moment, all possible futures open to her, all possible pasts lived and survived.

She watched Petridis struggle through the sand, and knew, seeing her retreat, she'd broken the woman far more completely than if she'd held a gun to her head and pulled the trigger, because she'd taken her son away from her again.

"I had no idea. I'm so sorry."

"You talk too much, Jude. There's no need to talk about anything."

TWENTY ONE

"Well, well…"

Sir Charles Wyndham's tone was difficult to decipher.

He sat in his wheelchair at the head of the conference table in the Crucible – the debriefing room – watching the news footage of Maria Petridis's arrest. Reports of the recovery of the legendary Golden Fleece were rife.

The dirt Jude had unearthed about the matriarch was *almost* as dramatic.

"The boy done good," Orla said, offering him an affectionate smile. Her arm was in a sling. She'd needed stitches on the knife wounds to her forearm, but all things considered she was feeling a lot better than she expected to.

There was no morning sickness for one thing.

Upon returning to Nonesuch, Jude Lethe had set to work on an archaeological dig of his own. It had taken time, but he wasn't about to emerge from the Nest before he had what he was looking for—proof of the woman's own confession, incontrovertible proof that she had in no small part helped engineer the Greek financial crisis for personal gain, making the country dependent on EU bailouts. Her second boast was that she also possessed the capacity to rescue the country when the time was right.

That she was found trying to flee the country with the legendary artefact, one of the last true treasures of her people. That was the icing on her particularly corrupt cake.

"It would seem that thanks to the pair of you the Argo Initiative has failed," the old man noted.

"Did you find out the significance of the Grey Sisters?" Orla asked, referring to the old women on the logo of the knitting company.

"Descendants of Jason's line. They were part of a project started by the Prussian Academy of Science and was continued by the German Berlin-Brandenurgische der Wissen Schaften. I must admit, it was quite a messy operation. AI co-partnered with them. They were Maria's co-conspirators, if you like, but their plans went far beyond reinstating the Greek monarchy. Plans that are now in ruins."

The hands of the grandfather clock ticked away steadily, the only sound in the room as they sat in silence.

Sir Charles cleared his throat. "Mr Lethe, would you be so kind as to excuse us?" he asked Jude graciously. "We will discuss your unexpected and completely irresponsible trip to Greece at a later time. And the bill for that hotel room of yours." The old man didn't look amused.

Jude rose slowly from his seat, wincing as his broken ribs caught. Sheepishly, he stole a glance at Orla. "Want to meet after this?"

"Sure." She smiled up at him.

"Ewell Village?"

"I'll see you there."

As Jude walked past his mentor and employer, Sir Charles offered his hand. "Contrary to how it may look, I am very proud of you, my boy," he said.

"Yes, Sir," Jude shook his hand and left them alone.

Sir Charles waited until he had closed the door before asking Orla, "How are you?"

"I'm fine," she said, too quickly for the old man to buy what she was selling.

He moved his wheelchair away from the screen and made his way around to Orla. Leaning forward, he reached for her hand.

"Orla, I ask you not as an employer, but as a friend."

"Honestly, I'm fine," she lied.

"Perhaps you are, perhaps you aren't. I want to tell you something." He squeezed her hand tight. "You may think me the sentimental old fool, but I've come to think of you as the daughter I never had." Orla resisted the urge to smile. She knew about Camila Morais, his adopted daughter who had died in the process of trying to leverage Nazi-built nuclear weapons into a new superpower. She held his gaze. "Maybe I am softening in my old age," he continued.

Orla couldn't help the smile that formed then, but the tear in her eye fell unchecked.

She gazed down at their hands.

His were scarred and pitted with trials she couldn't possibly imagine. Light brown liver spots had staked their claim on his pale skin. His nails, though neatly manicured as any gentleman's should be, were ridged with vitamin deficiency and slightly yellowed. Hers, in stark contrast, were young and smooth, olive toned. They barely hinted at the horrors she had endured with a small scrape or bruise here and there. The contrast made her think of life and death. The old man wouldn't be here forever. But then neither would she.

She stole a glance towards one of the marble statuettes standing on a plinth across the room – the statue of Ares, the

Greek God of War. "Is it crazy to think that I might have loved him, given time?" She wiped the tear away and forced a laugh.

"Of course it's possible. But for a while I think you might find yourself feeling sad, not just for the young man that died, but for all of the possible futures that died with him on that island. This life we lead isn't for everyone. And even those of us who live it well don't often look beyond tomorrow, certainly never as far as the happily ever after."

He ran the back of his fingers lightly against her cheek. He offered her a smile before releasing her hand and backing the wheelchair away to his usual spot at the head of the table.

"Obviously a holiday wasn't the best idea," he said with a wry smile.

"You think?"

"I want you to continue seeing the counsellor. Mr Frost sees him regularly, although don't tell him I said that. He likes to talk. I think it's his Irish blood. But, believe me, it always does one good to talk about the trials one has faced. Did wonders for me after Canary Wharf. You will go crazy if you dwell on the unchangeable past and those tiny but pivotal decisions we make or don't make that have the power to shape our world. The past is another country. We can only live in the present. We move on."

Orla stood, straightening her jacket. "Way ahead of you," she said.

Exiting the Crucible, she made her way across the wide wood-panelled entrance lobby where the old man's chess board was set up for the game he was playing against Maxwell.

She emerged from the Manor house into the warm Surrey air, the sun shining down on her. It would have been easy to be content. But there was work to be done. There was always work to be done.

A taxi pulled up alongside the stone portico.

"Where to?" the driver asked as she clambered in.

"Ewell Village."

*

Jude sat at a table for two in the corner of a quiet artisanal café. It was Orla's favourite spot in the village. Dressed casually in a navy blue long-sleeved shirt and blue jeans, he sipped at a cinnamon frothed cappuccino. A thick slice of frosted carrot cake was untouched on the plate beside it. Catching sight of her, he straightened in his seat and placed his cup on the table.

"Starting without me?" Orla asked as she reached him.

"The cake is too damned good," he stood and air-kissed both of her cheeks, wincing against the flare of pain in his ribs as he sat back down.

She ordered a latte and a few moments later the owner brought the coffee over to their table.

"Thank you." Orla held up her glass, they *chinked*. "To us. May we always be whatever it is we are."

"Ogmios." Jude said. And he was right, above and beyond anything else, that was exactly what they were. "You know when Koni's getting back from Poland?"

"The old man expects him in tomorrow."

"Good. I miss the bastard. It's been months since I last saw him, what with Peru, him in Poland, and then this."

"Don't take this the wrong way, Jude, but if you get it into your head to leave Nonesuch again and come racing out into the middle of nowhere to save the day I'm going to kill you. And it won't be pleasant. Understood?"

"Yeah," he agreed. "Getting my hands dirty just isn't my thing. Frankly I'm not sure I'm cut out for it."

"You think? What gave you that idea?"

"Nearly dying. Several times."

"Yeah, try not to do that again."

Standing before him, she leaned down, her face inches from his. Cupping his cheek in her hand, she softly kissed him on the lips.

She didn't have to tell him that the first time that she kissed him would also be the last.

When she pulled away, she stared into his eyes and whispered, "Thank you. For everything."

"It's what I do," he said. "And if you ever want to talk—"

"It's not what I do," she said, picking up the fork to steal his cake.

THE END

THE OGMIOS DIRECTIVE

Crucible

Steven Savile & Steve Lockley

Solomon's Seal

Steven Savile & Steve Lockley

Lucifer's Machine

Steven Savile & Rick Chesler

Wargod

Steven Savile & Sean Ellis

Shining Ones

Steven Savile & Richard Salter

Argo

Steven Savile & Ashley Knight

Lightning Source UK Ltd.
Milton Keynes UK
UKOW05f0319220417
299676UK00006B/66/P